NO FORGIVENESS

NO FORGIVENESS

A Novel By

HELEN NICKOLSON

Adelaide Books
New York / Lisbon
2018

No Forgiveness
a novel
by Helen Nickolson

Published by Adelaide Books, New York / Lisbon
adelaidebooks.org

Editor-in-Chief
Stevan V. Nikolic

For any information, please address Adelaide Books
at info@adelaidebooks.org
or write to:
Adelaide Books
244 Fifth Ave. Suite D27
New York, NY, 10001

ISBN13: 978-1-949180-01-5
ISBN10: 1-949180-01-8

Printed in the United States of America

Chapter One

How could she wash herself of the blood and the semen? How could she cleanse herself of the betrayal? Would the memories of being raped and sodomized ever leave her mind or would they always be entrapped in her subconscious to present themselves in nightmares? Yes, the physical pain would eventually go away, but the mental anguish would never disappear. She knew that for a fact, and she shuddered at what her life would now become. She knew she was to blame for what had happened because she had been so stupid—so, so stupid to allow herself to trust those who should be trustworthy but weren't. All her life she had trusted so readily, so easily, and consistently she had been hurt and disappointed. She thought that something must be wrong with her to never learn from the painful lessons that had steadily followed her from early childhood, but she was an optimist and her heart went out to others too easily.

She had just been warned by her own mother that same day, before her mother left to visit a sick relative, to stay far away from Ophelia and, now, she could blame no one but herself for not having listened. Her mother had earnestly and sadly explained, "You, your sister, and all your siblings are special to me. I love you all, but I can also see that you are very different from the others, and you must learn to protect yourself! I hate to say this, but I have eyes and have seen you struggle to be loved and accepted especially by your older sister Ophelia. I'm sorry to tell you that this will never happen since, for whatever reason, she took an immediate dislike to you when you were born. Perhaps this dislike is normal when two daughters are born so close to each other, and the older feels jealous at no longer being the center of attention. I don't know, but I have seen Ophelia rage at you and don't think she can control it any more than when the two of you were only children. I'm afraid that she would again push you into the fireplace as she did when you were only one, but she knows that you would be able to physically defend yourself now. No, I'm afraid that she will do something more warped than that, something that will hurt your soul instead of your body. Listen, I'm telling you this so harshly because I have to leave for one day and one night, and I don't want you to let your guard down!"

Despite the warning, she hadn't taken her mother's words to heart. Her mother had always protected her and, in her own way, had caused Ophelia to be even more unkind and jealous of her. She had even defended her sister occasionally to let Ophelia know how much she cared for her and how much she wanted to be friends. However, no matter how hard she tried, nothing seemed to gain her favor with Ophelia. Ophelia would simply look at her and taunt her by saying, "Do you think I'm stupid you little twit? I see how you kiss up to everyone and know you're just trying to kiss up to me. You want the neighbors to say that you're not only prettier but also nicer. Ha! Your time will come when you'll wish you had never been born."

Having heard her mother's warning and having heard Ophelia's evil words more than once, she now realized that she had been stupidly immature to trust Ophelia. She had been told more than once to not go anywhere alone with her older sister. But how could anyone have truly expected that her sister would so callously turn her over to that brute Giorgio? He had always been a brute, and he had so cruelly misused her—her body and her reputation. Everyone knew him and his family; everyone knew of their cruelty and heartlessness and disregard for others. The parents had earned their reputation and they had trained him to be as cruel and heartless as they were themselves. Those horrible people were a scourge and embarrassment to their villagers and to the entire Greek nation! Never would she have considered him for her future bridegroom and her mother would never have approved of her marrying him, as she made obvious when he stopped by their house the previous month to ask for her hand in marriage.

Her mother had been polite to Giorgo and offered him a cup of coffee, a glass of water, and some gliko as she would have to any guest in their house. This was the custom and good manners were expected regardless of how one may have left about their company. However, upon hearing of Giorgo's request, her mother was barely able to hold down the bile that leaped to her throat, and Giorgo was astute enough to comprehend how reprehensible the thought was to her. He was insulted, but he believed in his ability to get whatever he wanted and thought to himself, "All right Old Lady, you may not want me, but I will get the prize whether you approve or not. I know how to make things happen, and you will not stand in my way."

So, yes, she had known that Giorgo wanted her since both she and Ophelia had overheard the conversation. Actually, they had eavesdropped from the adjoining bedroom, which wasn't hard to do since there were only two rooms in the house that their father had built. There was the sleeping area that the women shared, and there was the living area where her brothers slept and also worked as the living room and kitchen. It was there that Ophelia had thrown her into the fireplace.

Neither she nor Ophelia said much upon hearing Giorgo declare his love for her although both of them knew that he should have been asking for Ophelia's hand since she was the older of the two. Ophelia merely grimaced and muttered that she wouldn't have wanted him if he had asked for her, but she knew that Ophelia felt the insult and there was nothing anyone could say to make her feel better.

She hadn't really paid any attention or given Giorgo the time of day before his proposal and she didn't act any differently after. She had her own dreams and desires and Giorgo was simply irrelevant to her. He was not part of her life and never would be. In her mind, he would look elsewhere and find someone else and stop thinking about her. He wasn't bad looking and some might even consider him handsome in a coarse kind of way. There had been talk about his availability and not all of the young women had feared him or his family despite their reputation. Some of them even considered him desirable in a risqué fashion.

She, however, was a very naïve seventeen-year-old in the little village of Kato Kourouni in Evia, Greece, which had approximately two hundred people. Born on October 10,

1901, or so her mother thought since no birth records were kept for females, she hadn't ventured far from the village and had no desire to do so. She loved the lush, green landscape and mountainous terrain and, despite the physically hard daily life she and everyone had to endure, she looked forward to every day whether it was working out in the fields or in the house. Washing clothes was especially hard since she had to walk down a steep pathway to reach the spring with abundant water, but again, she didn't mind. That's where she could talk and laugh with the other women and catch up on the latest news from those who had visited other villages. The very worst part about her life, in her mind, was that they had to use an outdoor area several yards from the house to relieve themselves, but she hadn't experienced anything else so having the pit latrine didn't preoccupy her. It wasn't really worth thinking about.

The picturesque village of Kato Kourouni was in central Evia on a mountain slope with poor soil for farming but a striking terrain and lush vegetation where she would be content to live the rest of her life—with the right man of course. Katerina hadn't seen much of the world and didn't expect to. She didn't really even care about the rest of the world and didn't feel it could offer her anything better than what she at home. It was 1919 and World War I had been over for almost a year, and she was happy that no more Greek men would need to die. They had already lost about 5,000 and Greeks were tired of wars and fighting. Katerina and her family felt so lucky that neither of her brothers had been old enough to fight in the war, but they also felt guilty that some of their neighbors had lost sons; the grief on the parents' faces was etched deeply and reflected the mourning in their hearts. To Katerina, it was incredulous that anyone would fight to death and be so cruel to fellow human beings. For that, she prayed every Sunday that the world would become a better place, and she lit a candle for those who had died so needlessly.

Whenever she thought of Giorgo, which was very infrequently, she couldn't understand why he would even want her. It was obvious that she wasn't interested in him, so she had figured that he would get the message and just leave her alone. Didn't he have any pride? He should have realized and not have humiliated himself by asking for her. She had never even looked him directly in the face although the face was handsome. Whenever she had crossed paths with him, she had kept her eyes downcast and had moved out of his path as quickly as possible. No matter how handsome some thought him to be, she wasn't interested. She had sensed his evil and sly nature and had stayed out of his sight as much as possible. The one and only time she had shaken his hand, she had felt nasty vibrations zip through her arm and immediately afterward washed her hands with soap.

On the other hand, Michael, the man of her dreams, from a nearby village is the one she loves and has loved for several years. Everyone always spoke so well of him, and he was not only handsome but also sweet. His eyes lit up whenever he saw her, and he, unlike the typical Greek male, treated her as an equal although she, like most girls, hadn't been allowed to go to school; he talked to her of events taking place in the world and Greece, discussed why Greece had even entered the wretched war, and, most importantly, always treated her with respect. He had never touched her other than to politely shake her hand, and the rumor was that he was going to ask her family for permission to marry her. She had heard that and hoped with all her heart it was true.

They would make a good couple in both looks and temperament. They were both hard-working, honest, and kind. He was tall and fine-looking with broad shoulders, muscular arms, and long legs that she imagined were also muscular. His eyes were also dark and usually had a twinkle that reflected his quick amusement with whatever life dared present him. He was ready to deal with the world, to be just but to also defend what was his. His hair was dark and curly and she knew he would never become bald although she would love him even if he did. But she was an equal match and turned heads easily whenever she entered a room or passed by a table of men at the local kafenio where the men went for coffee or a drink every afternoon. That's where they talked politics and thought they were going to solve the problems of the world although they pretty much said the same things day after day while their wives worked at home. Her body was long for a woman of her era and her curves were curvaceously distributed in a Rubenesque fashion with an ample bosom, small waist, and rounded hips. Her hair was jet black, her skin milky white, and her eyes a deep green. She knew she was a knock-out and proudly held her shoulders back and her back straight.

Giorgo, like most men young and old, had been struck by her beauty. He desired her and lusted for her. He had truly thought that her mother would agree to his proposal of marriage and that he would have this gorgeous woman in his bed to do with as he wished night after night. He wanted her so much that he had offered to forfeit the dowry that typically went with the bride. That he had gone beyond what any other man would do only made his embarrassment at the rejection more unbearable. Now that his dreams had been dashed, he still desired Katerina but thought she was arrogant in how she displayed and carried herself. He wanted to teach her a lesson and wondered if her sister might help him. After all, word had gotten around that Ophelia was jealous and unhappy that Katerina got all the attention.

Katerina had had no inkling of what had been going through Giorgo's mind. She walked through her day with her head in the clouds thinking only of Michael and their future. But now, after what Giorgo had done to her, how could marriage with Michael take place? It would be a miracle if Michael could understand and accept what had happened without blaming her. She had lost her innocence because of Giorgo and Ophelia and could no longer expect Michael to want her. He, like all other men, desired a virgin on his wedding night and she no longer had virginity to offer him. She, the trusting idiot, had so easily been misled by her sister and knew that no man other than the brutish barbarian Giorgo would have anything to do with her in the future. She needed to survive his assault but could neither comprehend nor deny what had happened since it had occurred just a few hours earlier. Katerina found it too hard to think and felt herself starting to shake. Panic was taking over and she could sense her body starting to shut down. She had been attacked so horribly, so viciously! And, she knew that she would have to marry Georgio to maintain her honor and that of her family's, especially since her father had died two years earlier and she had no male relatives old enough to protect her. But she didn't want miserable Giorgo with his heavy, hard hands and forceful penis which he had used as a weapon against her. The thought of him ever touching her again made her stomach churn and brought a sourness to her throat, but she knew that she didn't have time to get sick. There would be plenty of time to vomit later.

In order to focus and stay in the present, she spoke to herself out loud in a scared but determined voice, "Katerina, you must get out of here before that bastard comes back and does the same things all over. You need to get out of this dirty little pigsty of a hut that he dragged you into. You saw what a cruel animal he is and he'll only hurt you again if he finds you here." He had been so cruel and hurt her so badly when he pushed himself into her, over and over, without any regard for her inexperience, her virginity, and her innocence. It had especially hurt when he went after her from the back.

If she could only find some water and a cloth, she could at least wipe off his scent and the physical evidence of his abuse. Yes, she thought, she could do that and then somehow escape back to her own home. She knew she had to get out quickly and said over and over to herself: "Katerina, concentrate! You need to get out. Don't become hysterical now. Keep your wits about you and you will find the way."

At the same time, she desperately wondered if she could keep this shame a secret, but, deep down, she knew that her sister wouldn't let her do that.

"Oh, my sister," she cried. "How could you have handed me over so easily? We are of the same blood but it meant nothing to you. I wish you had killed me somehow without my ever knowing how much you hate me. You know that death would have been easier for me than this." That betrayal, her sister's, was worse than any of the physical torture she had been through and tears ran hotly down Katerina's cheeks. She had been taught by her mother and father that family was supposed to love each other, protect each other, and be loyal to each other above all else. But Ophelia had always acted strangely toward her and, in her gut, she had always recognized Ophelia's hostility. Perhaps it was because of their looks.

Because of comments she had heard, Katerina had always known that she was beautiful and that her sister was not very attractive. They resembled each other a bit, but Katerina was light and evenly toned while Ophelia was dark and somewhat splotchy; Katerina was tall and shapely while Ophelia was squat and plump; Katerina walked lightly and gracefully on her toes while Ophelia sort of shuffled along a little bent over. Katerina had felt the jealousy oozing from Ophelia daily and had always tried to be extra kind to her sister. It just hadn't made any difference. She had had to pay for her beauty. Inwardly, she had always known that Ophelia had despised her from the time of her birth. Ophelia had been envious of Katerina's beauty and kindness, and it must have been fate that she would lead Katerina to this monster Giorgo for him to destroy any chances of happiness that she had in this world. As these thoughts ran through her head and emotions raged in her heart, Katerina found it even more depressing knowing that Ophelia probably felt justified in her actions and triumphant in tricking her.

Through unchecked tears, Katerina remembered how Ophelia had come into the house that same morning with a smile on her face and suggested that they go together to the August 15th festival in another little village only two miles away. "Come Katerina, our mother isn't here but there's no reason for us not to go to the dance. We'll have to walk there, but we can do that in a about an hour or so at the most. I'll even let you use some of my powder because I don't think I've been very nice to you lately." She knew how much Katerina loved to dance and how hard it would be for her to refuse going to a festival. Festivals and celebrations is what they all looked forward to. There wasn't much else in the little mountainous villages of Evia to be excited about. Life was very difficult and the days were full of work either in the house or in the fields.

Katerina felt so warm and happy that Ophelia wanted to spend time with her and agreed quickly to go to the festival. Their mother's warning vacated her mind immediately, and the two sisters left around 7:00 PM on the warm August night. As they briskly walked along anticipating the evening, or sometimes just sauntered like the teenagers they were, Katerina thought wistfully that perhaps she and her sister had entered into another, better stage of caring. She wanted her sister's companionship so much and hoped their future would be friendlier. Even when a sigh of the warning penetrated her thoughts, she brushed it aside.

They had both dressed to the best of their wardrobes and giggled together thinking of the young men who would be there. They had carefully coiffed their hair and put on just a tiny bit of rouge on their cheeks and lips. They knew they couldn't flirt too much since they would be talked about, but they also knew that you don't have to speak to flirt. A dance done gracefully is more flirtatious than sweet words spoken and Katerina in particular was well aware of that. She could barely contain her excitement thinking that Michael would most likely be there—it was after all his village that they were going to. They would probably dance the sirto, the most common line dance throughout Greece, and she could touch him by holding his hand as the line dance circled the floor; there was nothing inappropriate about that since they had to hold hands for this dance and definitely nothing that anyone could gossip about.

The sisters walked up the sloped narrow dirt road toward Ano Kourouni, the sister village to Kato Kourouni which was called "Ano" because it was located at a higher location. Sometimes they jumped into a song and sometimes they just chatted about their dreams. Katerina was just naturally excited and felt especially high-spirited. Ophelia seemed more nervous than excited, but knowing that her sister tended to be a worry wart, Katerina didn't pay much attention.

The Greek countryside, unlike some of the Cycladic stark islands, was opulent in this part of the country and it was such a pleasure to smell the mountain tea plants growing along the road. The evening air held such promise of romance and mystery. The sisters talked of love, of marriage, of children. Being thoroughly inexperienced, they couldn't talk of kissing or sex or anything physical to do with a man. Actually, Katerina couldn't help but think of what it might feel like to kiss Michael. What a handsome man, she thought. He was so dark and tall with a physique and muscles that showed the hours he spent working in the fields, and she blushed at the thought of him lying in bed next to her naked. She thought about the beautiful children they could make together and how much she would love them. She had no clue that Ophelia was thinking of the same man and blushing at the same thoughts. She had also heard the rumors that he wanted to marry her sister, and she was going to do everything she could to stop it.

Halfway to their destination, Katerina realized that the route they were taking was not the regular way to Ano Kourouni. She had been talking and daydreaming too much and hadn't been paying any attention to the direction they were taking. "Ophelia," she said, "Why are we going through these fields? Don't you remember the way? You know, all we're going to do is ruin our shoes and that would be a shame since we only have one good pair each. We've walked to Ano Kourouni so many times that we should know the road in our sleep. Maybe I distracted us too much with my silly conversation."

"Oh, Katerina, this is just a shortcut. I know where we're going. Come on, you've been this way before and it's so much shorter than the regular road. With this shortcut, we'll have even more energy to dance all night. Really, I'm surprised that you don't remember the way through these fields."

"Okay, although I really don't remember having gone this way before. But, you know me. I often don't look where I'm going."

She had expected a chuckle from Ophelia, but instead Ophelia suddenly stopped, leaned forward from her waist and said how tired and thirsty she had become. She did look awfully pale and unsteady. Of course, becoming lightheaded and needing water made sense on a warm August evening, but when Ophelia suggested that they stop at the vacant, rundown house by the road to see if the well still worked, Katerina had a strange foreboding and didn't want to stop there at all.

"You know," she said to Ophelia, "that house has been empty since the Marakou family left for America and that well is probably dry. Let's just go on a bit more slowly and we can get some fresh water when we reach the festival. We've been walking for quite a while and can't be more than ten minutes away from Ano Kourouni. Besides, there are probably snakes or scorpions around that well, and I'm so terrified of those ugly creatures."

"I should have known that would be your response" was Ophelia's retort. "You've been so pleasant today that I thought you had changed, but I can see that you're as selfish as always. All I'm asking is for an additional five minutes to get some water because I'm so thirsty, but all you can think of is that people will admire your dancing and you want to show off as much and for as long as possible. Your own sister's feelings and health don't concern you. Well, maybe I'll just stop by myself and you can continue without me."

Oh, what shame Katerina felt—especially since she knew that there was some truth to the comment! She did indeed love to dance and was vain enough to enjoy the compliments people always gave her. She was anxious to get to the festival and hear the music. But she should have been thinking of her sister. Yes, Ophelia was right. She had spoken out of selfishness, and was mortified that she could be so self-centered. People were right in saying she was spoiled and had been favored by both her mother and father. With this sorrow in her heart, all she could do was to hang her head and apologize to Ophelia. Of course, the only right thing to do was to stop.

They carefully walked to the crumbling well side-stepping potholes and looking for snakes and scorpions, and as they stood by the side of the well against the chipped stone, Katerina suddenly felt two strong, muscular arms grab her from behind. Shock waves went through her body and fear overcame all other emotions. No one had the right to grab her in this manner; she was a young woman who deserved respect; this is not how men treated her. This must be a vagrant travelling through the area who had the temerity to act insolently.

She wanted to scream but no sound came out of her throat. She froze and looked for help to Ophelia. However, Ophelia's face had hardened and the look in her eyes had nothing of compassion in it; instead, the look was gloating and sly. A look that said there's nothing for you in my heart, and I'm finally going to make sure that you get what you deserve. A look that said your dreams will become fairytales, and my fairytales will turn into dreams and reality. Ophelia turned and ran and left Katerina without a word.

"No! No, Ophelia! Don't leave me like this!" Katerina screamed. "I am your sister and I love you. Don't desert me like this. Please."

The iron arms pulled her unresponsive, semi-frozen body into the little house and the man spoke: "So you've thought you're too good for me, huh? You have your sights set on that idiot Michael and think you can insult me by ignoring me. You bitch! Your life after tonight will be changed forever and, whether you marry me or not, no one else will want to touch you. They will know that you're a whore and that you came to me willingly. Your sister will attest to that and more. Just see what Michael will say to you if you go to him for help. No matter how much you beg, he will no longer want you."

She then knew that it was Giorgo who gripped her and knew that she would be screaming and crying for mercy before he finished with her. What she didn't know was that the pain would be so great that she would pass out before she could really beg. Thank God, she didn't know what to expect. The rape was thorough and brutal the first time and every time after that. She stopped counting and believing there was no way that he could continue much longer because she had been wrong more than once.

More than once she beseeched God, the Virgin Mary, and the saints, "Please have him finish soon, soon, soon," and then mercifully passed out. The very last time that she passed out, he couldn't revive her and finally left. She heard later that he had gone to the festival and danced for hours. He had danced with Ophelia leading the syrto line dance while Katerina lay in a heap on the cement floor of the old shack.

When she finally came to, she was shuddering and in shock, hurting everywhere but feeling nothing. She could only sense that he was no longer there, but she knew that he might return--no, that he would definitely return. She positively had to get out of the house and labored to put her limbs into motion, meanwhile making a stab with her torn clothes at wiping his filthy semen and smell off her.

Water and a cloth. She needed to find that. She needed to get the stains off her and go home to her own bed. To her own bed where she might find sanity again. Yes, yes, she felt the cloth in the dark and found a little water in a nearby jug to scrape gently at her vagina, anus, and legs.

This was the ultimate in betrayal. Not even an enemy would have led her into this trap. How could a sister? No cloth could scrape away the wound inside her heart and soul; no salve could soften the sharp jaggedness there. But she would survive. If, at the worst, she was forced to marry him, she would find a manner of revenge. If she didn't have to marry him, she would still find a manner of revenge. Katerina made her cross and prayed to God to forgive her for whatever she might do. She prayed forgiveness for being willing to go to hell if necessary. After all, she had already experienced hell and hadn't been lucky enough to have simply died.

Chapter Two

Whimpering and mostly naked, she half crawled, half stumbled her way back home. She found a long stick along the way and used it to steady her balance since the countryside was rocky and potholes were common. She fell a couple of times and used the stick for support to stand again. The morning dew helped her keep her consciousness. The smell of mountain tea was still in the air, but she no longer felt any pleasure in the scent. Tears trickled slowly down her face, but she wasn't even aware of them. Katerina knew that she needed the safety of her own house, her bed, and the loving touch of her mother. Her mother would have come in last night and would be worrying about her, pacing around the house and sensing that Ophelia had carried out some devilish plan.

"Mama, I'm on my way home. I'm hurt but I'll make it. Oh Mama, send me some strength," she cried to herself. "You were so right and I didn't listen to you, so I know I deserve to be punished. But Mama, it shouldn't be like this. Please, please forgive me. You're the only one who will still love me after I've dishonored the family in such a terrible way. I just didn't know or expect anything this bad to happen to me. I love you Mama."

Finally, she saw the blurry outline of the stone, unassuming house her father had built and reached the steep cement stairs that went to the second floor; from relief at finally having arrived, it looked like a heavenly palace to her. The first floor, which had a cobbled courtyard, was somewhat of a stable or barn where they kept the donkey, two goats, and one lamb. More goats and some sheep would have been welcome if they could have afforded to buy and also feed them. They couldn't. They had always just managed to scrape by, but after Katerina's father died, life had become more difficult. She heard the animals move around but couldn't make any of the friendly sounds or words that she normally had for them. Her lips were as battered as her body and her throat was raspy and sore from all the screams that had forced themselves through it earlier.

The house was typical of the poor, village houses of the time period: whitewashed stone, sharp narrow steps without a guard to help someone climb up or down, a dangerously small porch at the top that one could easily slip of, animals at ground level, and a couple of rooms upstairs. It was nothing fancy, but they were proud of it since Katerina's father had built it himself, and it had survived several light earthquakes, which were common to all of Greece. They were simple people who didn't require much and were thankful for good health, especially since her father had died of pneumonia. They prayed for good health and thanked God for watching over them. They had no running water or electricity or an indoor bathroom, but they were thankful for the few things they had and let God know every day.

On hands, knees, and raw, outstretched arms, she navigated her body by clinging to the steps all the way up to the main little porch at the top, and then she barely managed to stand and open the door. The door squeaked slightly but enough to let her mother know that she was home. Her mother, obviously worried, ran toward her to make sure that she was okay but then jumped back clasping her hands over her heart in fright. "My eyes, my sweetheart, what happened to you? Did you fall down a cliff and hurt yourself or did someone do this to you? You have blood and bruises on you. Your clothes are torn and you look so frantic. What happened? Ophelia told me that you were going to go to the festival with her, but, instead, you disappeared, and she gave up waiting for you. You should never have gone by yourself. We can trust our neighbors in the village, but you never know who else might be out there and do you harm."

"Mama, please help me to clean up and I will tell you a very different story from Ophelia's. You were right about her but I didn't listen to you. Like an idiot, I trusted her. Please help me. I feel so weak and hurt so much. Oh Mama, I don't understand how she could have helped Giorgo do this to me."

Silently grieving to see her child in such pain, her mother gathered water and old towels. She found some salve in a chest that held herbs and medicinal supplies, and then, very slowly, helped Katerina to undress. As she took Katerina's torn dress off her, she could tell what had happened and tears welled up in her eyes. Her sobs racked her body and she trembled at what she saw. Her beautiful, naive child had been molested, and all she could offer to soothe her daughter was love, soft kisses, a little bit of broth, bread, and water. She kept murmuring to herself, "If I could only take the pain from her." She wanted to pull the pain out of Katerina's body and swallow it herself, but knew that pain couldn't be transferred to her regardless of her wishes. Bitterly and with great remorse, she recognized that Ophelia had played a pivotal role in this sad event and wished she'd never had that first daughter who could so jealously inflict sorrow on her sister. She wanted to curse Ophelia and damn her to hell but her strong religious beliefs held her back. God would not approve of such words.

The next afternoon the three of them talked. Katerina had awakened close to noon after sleeping poorly on her little cot, and her body ached everywhere despite the salve that her mother had swabbed so liberally over her entire frame. It was very difficult, if not almost impossible, for her to have Ophelia sit across the table and to hear her deny her culpability. She finally saw her sister for the evil person she had always been and wanted no further association with her. She was no longer the child who had always tried to humor and coax Ophelia into kindness. She no longer cared.

Ophelia made it obvious that she felt no responsibility, no guilt and blamed Katerina for leading Giorgo, and, according to her, other men, on with her dancing and her mischievous, teasing looks. She stated her opinion coldly and without hesitation: "How can you expect men to not feel invited or excited if you dance like that?" she questioned. "You've had no shame in your behavior. They believe that you're welcoming them to share much more than a look when you strut in front of the kafenio and actually talk to them. The kafenio is a male haven for coffee or drinks and any woman who goes by on a regular basis is obviously inviting the wrong attention. I refuse to take the blame for your behavior Katerina! You needed to be taught a lesson and I'm glad that you were."

Nevertheless, the basic truth of the betrayal could not be repudiated, and their mother decided that Ophelia would be sent to a cousin in a nearby town for an undetermined length of time. Until she left, Ophelia vehemently refuted that she had had any role in leading her sister to Giorgo, even though she felt some shame when she saw how ravaged Katerina looked; she might have felt enough remorse to not again look at Katerina after that first long and stunned stare at her bruised body and face. What had obviously happened was not exactly what she had expected, at least not at the level of crudeness and the callousness of Giorgo's attack. Being just as sexually innocent as Katerina, Ophelia had not envisioned this ghastly outcome. She had thought that Giorgo was in love with Katerina and wanted to express his romantic feelings. She had also thought that Giorgo might charm Katerina into sexual intercourse, but she had never expected what was obviously repeated and punishing rape. In any case, she insisted to herself that she wasn't responsible since Giorgo had told her that he merely wanted to talk to Katerina alone.

Weeks passed and Katerina's bruises slowly healed. She didn't miss Ophelia at all and was comfortable being alone with her mother. Her white skin returned to its even, delicate creamy white color. Her green eyes became clear, and her black hair regained its shiny sheen. She was without doubt again a striking beauty: tall, long-limbed, rounded with lovely curves, and a straight, elegant posture.

She still had nightmares but slept with her mother and was calmed by her whenever she woke up trembling or screaming. She hadn't left the house the entire time, so no one had seen her to ask questions about her appearance. Her mother, Kyria Maria, simply said that she had had a little injury and had to stay indoors. No company was allowed to see her because she apparently had a slight fever or a little of this and a little of that. People knew something terribly wrong had taken place, but they had enough respect for the widow and her dead husband to not burden her with many questions.

As she healed, the time came when Katerina felt she had to face what had occurred. She wanted to see Michael and tell him what had happened. He deserved to know the details in order to understand that she was not to blame. She loved him and hoped he loved her enough to still want to marry her. Michael had stopped by several times to ask about her, but her mother had stopped him in the yard and hadn't invited him in for coffee, so he knew as little as the neighbors about what had actually happened to her. Now, though, she felt she had to see him.

She couldn't go to his house by herself without causing talk and speculation about their relationship, so she asked her mother to accompany her. Yes, she no longer had her virginity, but she still wanted to act appropriately, respectfully and according to what was accepted as custom; she also needed to protect his reputation as an honorable man so she needed to be careful. He was a good man and would surely understand that the position she had been put into was nothing of her own doing. She would plead with him to not blame her for her stupidity and promise to stand by him and love him forever. He deserved that.

So, mother and daughter went to Ano Kourouni, where the August festival had been held, to talk with him on a light, cheerful morning. They walked arm in arm, obviously affectionate, somewhat nervous, and full of hope. Their faith in him was such that their steps were lighthearted, and they viewed the future with some consternation but mainly with confidence. "Mama, you did say that he loves me, didn't you? From what you said he was planning to ask for me in marriage any day. That's probably why he stopped by several times to see me in the last few weeks."

About an hour later, Michael saw them walking toward him from some distance. He normally would have been working in one of his fields but had decided to do some repairs around his house that morning, and they were lucky to find him at home. He was out in the yard cleaning around some bushes and trimming up the broad mulberry tree that provided wonderful afternoon shade. The villages were hot in September and shade was welcome as well as necessary. His muscles glistened in the sun and he looked like an ancient god. The sweat dripped off his back from the work and heat, but he had no idea that a woman could look at him and take her imagination to another level. In his mind, he looked fine but not anything beyond the ordinary.

He saw Kyria Maria and quickly put his shirt on. He was very conscious of propriety and in no manner wanted to offend other villagers or guests—especially women. He was surprised to see that she looked poorly as if she had lost five or more years of her life. She looked haggard and for her, since she was a good-sized woman, relatively frail. Katerina looked beautiful as always and he felt his heart miss a beat as he studied her. For him to contain his passion, he would need to marry her soon. He had tried to talk to her mother recently but Kyria Maria had been so subdued that he hesitated bringing up the topic. But it had been a while since he had seen Katerina, and his heart raced at the thought of them in the same house and the same bed, night after night making love and children. He had expected her at the dance on August fifteenth and waited around expectantly until he knew it would be too late for her to appear. He wanted to see her dance and to join her if only to hold her hand. Ophelia had noted his expression and his darting glances throughout the crowd as if he were looking for someone. She hadn't been pleased since she knew he was searching for Katerina. He had also seen Ophelia dancing with Giorgo right beside her and had wanted to warn her about Giorgo, but for some reason he kept his distance and didn't speak to her.

As the two women came closer, he thought that perhaps he would be able to gather his courage and ask for her hand today. He blushed and hardened at the thought of having her for his wife. The blush underlined the excitement of what could be and the anticipation of what would be. How fortuitous that they had come to Ano Kourouni today on an errand and had walked by his house. They must be planning to visit one of his neighbors he thought.

He greeted them with a "Kali Mera," Good Day, and stepped closer to shake hands. He couldn't help but observe that Katerina also looked somewhat frail and hoped that she wasn't feeling ill. "My dear Kyria Maria and Katerina, you both look as lovely as always, but I can't help but see that perhaps you've been working too hard and are a little bit pale. Please come inside so that I can offer you at least a glass of water. Although it's still morning, it's too warm to sit out here under the sun, and, Katerina, we don't want to burn that lovely complexion you have."

"Yes," they agreed and walked toward the door. "We would appreciate that glass of water and we have something serious to discuss with you. Perhaps you could spare an hour of your time."

He then realized that they weren't planning on visiting a neighbor and had come specifically to see him. Graciously, he ushered them upstairs to the little salon he had and offered them a glass of water and some orange glyko and kourambiethes, sweets that his mother had made and brought to him the day before.

"I know that you want to discuss a serious matter with me, so please go ahead and tell me what's on your minds. If I can help you in some way, I would be happy to do so," he offered while looking from one to the other unwaveringly but also curiously. "You probably want to discuss getting some extra help with the harvest this fall. I know you had good crops this year and I'm delighted that this will be a good year from you."

Katerina didn't know where to start or what to say and only looked at the floor. Neither did her mother know how to start and awkwardly fumbled, stopping and stuttering as she spoke, with the story of what had occurred to Katerina the previous month. As her mother explained, Katerina could feel the tears starting to burn in her eyes and she hung her head in humiliation. Instead of being on the receiving end of a marriage proposal, she and her mother were here to beg the man she loved to save her. She glanced at Michael but couldn't gauge his reaction since his face had closed off and his eyes had taken on a pained but somewhat icy and distant expression. Those were not the eyes she recognized and loved. She could see that he didn't want to show any emotion, but she didn't comprehend why. Of course, she thought, he was undoubtedly trying to think logically to solve the problem. He was, after all, a very intelligent man that people talked about having a future in politics. He might not reach the highest levels but exhibited a lot of promise.

Having told the story, Kyria Maria said, "I believe you have been in love with Katerina for years and were planning to ask for her in marriage. Without doubt, I know that Katerina has thought of no one other than you and her dreams for the future included only you as a husband."

Still, there was no response from Michael, and Kyria Maria didn't know what else to do but continue with, "She is still the same person. Yes, she has been horribly dishonored but her dreams are still of you. She was violated but did not bring this crime upon herself. Her only fault in all of this was that she was very gullible and trusting. Do you love her or did we come with mistaken ideas?"

Still there was no response from Michael. He only looked at them with a detached expression and dead eyes. Katerina knew she had to speak out in order to feel some connection with him. "Michael," she implored. "You know that we came to ask you to marry me and allow me to regain some of my pride and honor again. It is so much to ask, but perhaps you have enough feelings for me to accept me even though I am now impaired goods according to our society and villages. I know that marrying me may cause you pain at times because people talk and gossip unkindly. I may also be an impediment to your career and ambitions. But, please accept that I will try so hard to make you happy and to be the best wife you could ever have. I will love you and cherish you as my husband beyond your imagination. I love you now and will regardless of what may happen in the future. Will you marry me?"

He had no choice at this point but to reply with what he found in his mind and heart, and that was convoluted. He understood that she had suffered greatly and wished that he could spear a knife straight into Giorgo's black heart. He knew she had been blameless in this abominable episode. But, he wondered if he could believe that one sister had so easily betrayed the other; he had never heard of such a thing before and found it hard to grasp. He was sure that Katerina would never have gone to Giorgo willingly, but he could understand how Giorgo might somehow have misconstrued her demeanor or her mannerisms. She was, after all, a natural flirt and might be trying to blame Ophelia unfairly. If he married her, he would be the laughing stock of the area and he had definite ideas of what position he wanted to hold in the village and perhaps on a wider basis. Just last week, someone had suggested that he consider running for mayor of Ano Kourouni. With Katerina, no one would take him seriously any longer. Yes, she was lovely, but marriage had to have a better foundation than looks alone. Yes, marriage had to go beyond romantic notions.

He had to have the right woman as his wife. After all, he had others than himself to think about: his family and future children. He knew that Katerina was a victim, but he was certain that Ophelia had become a victim also. With marriage, one had to have clear expectations and be practical. He used the logic he had been taught and emphasized the general mandate of the system that he had grown up in.

"I must tell you that my heart grieves for what you have had to bear Katerina. I hurt at the thought of what that scoundrel did to you. Women should be protected and cherished, and that's the relationship I wanted with you. However, I don't see myself capable of marrying you in these circumstances. For all I know, you may be carrying Giorgo's child and I could never accept his child as one of my own. I apologize and can't express my regret adequately, but I will light a candle especially for you every time I enter a church. I had such hopes for us and want you to know that I also will suffer. Under these circumstances, we need to think practically and assess the impact of our actions on our families and our future. The best advice that I can give you is to marry Giorgo and keep your faith in God. Pray to Him and he will show you mercy."

"Kyria Maria," he added, "I must say something more to all of this because I have always had such deep concern for you and your daughters. I simply cannot accept that Ophelia truly did what you accuse her of. Ophelia is just another innocent who deserves the best a man can give, and, having known her all of my life, I feel an obligation to her too. Although I haven't felt love for her in the same way as I have for Katerina, I have always cared for her. The only way that I can see to be of help to you and your family is to ask for Ophelia in marriage. In this manner, I can help you maintain your reputation and good name. Surely, if this could happen to Katerina, it could happen to Ophelia as well. If you agree to my proposal, I think we should have the marriage immediately and not tempt more wrath from God. Yes, I have had deep feelings for Katerina but I also have respect for our culture and norms. If I can help Katerina in the future, I will. However, I don't see that marriage with her is the solution here."

Before losing consciousness after hearing Michael utter these dreadful words, Katerina could only breathe out, "Mama, this will kill me, but do what is best for the family. I'm sure Ophelia also loves Michael and would be happy to be his wife. It will be difficult to bear but I understand. My heart will die, and, despite that, I will continue to live. I will breathe through my lungs but never again feel through my heart. If this is what Michael and Ophelia want, let it happen. I will stand in no one's way."

Kyria Maria heard her daughter and regarded Michael with a level of contempt she hadn't considered or experienced previously. He was not the man she had admired and respected, and she regretted having come to his house to beg. She was as stunned as Katerina at what Michael had said; but yes, his words held a level of truth and definite practicality. And she did have another child. At least if Ophelia married Michael, she would be settled in her own home and not bother them any longer. She would no longer hurt Katerina. She could only do her best to salvage the situation.

Gently, Kyria Maria wiped a wetted napkin over Katerina's face and touched her shoulders lightly to bring her back to wakefulness. She kissed Katerina ever so tenderly and said, "My love, we will do the right thing for the family. We will have this marriage and work through the pain together. Ophelia has been in love with Michael for many years and she will be delighted to agree to this arrangement. Whether you marry Giorgo or not is entirely up to you, and you need to remember that you will always have a home with me."

Kyria Maria then turned to Michael and curtly said, "We can have the wedding within the week if you want."

Chapter Three

The wedding took place three weeks later and Katerina attended along with numerous people from both Kato Kourouni and Ano Kourouni. The ceremony was late in the afternoon on Sunday, October twelfth, two days after her eighteenth birthday, which she had spent contemplating the easiest way to kill herself. She knew it would be a sin against God to commit suicide and that she would not be buried properly. She didn't really care about the burial but she was truly afraid of going to hell. Also, she didn't want her mother to suffer any more than she already had, so she decided that hell on earth would be preferable to hell after death and resigned herself to a joyless future. Time would pass and eventually she would meet her maker in good conscience.

That Sunday afternoon was lovely, soft and reflective with few clouds in the sky—a perfect day for a wedding. There was very little breeze, just enough to stir the leaves slightly. The day, however, felt flawed and a guarded silence had fallen throughout the village. Shadows lurked in the church yard like melancholy spirits held at bay. Even the church bells sounded ominous and several attendees felt a shiver cross their bones. It scared them enough to make the sign of the cross as if that might hold off any evil, and some even touched the blue eye trinket that they had in their pockets although believing in the power of the blue eye was considered a heathen practice by the church.

In the last week Katerina had helped with the baking of various Greek sweets—kourambiethes, baklava, and melo-makarouna--and had tried to be as cordial to her sister as she could stomach. It was not for love of Ophelia but for her own pride that she struggled to maintain her equanimity; she wanted no pity from Ophelia or from anyone who had expected that she, not Ophelia, would be the bride. Did she want to cry? To scream? To shout? To curse at the unfairness of it all? Yes, but Katerina had not cried again since the day they had gone to Michael's house. Her stomach would constrict with sudden spasms if she allowed herself to think of Michael, so she tried not to think of him. But sometimes she couldn't stop herself. Her mind wandered and questioned how he could so easily have become immune to her and willing to marry Ophelia instead. He didn't love Ophelia and they all knew it. But then, she realized, marriage doesn't necessarily require love. and having sex with Ophelia would not require love either. One woman could bear children as well as another, and, in the dark, one woman could substitute for another.

She had dressed carefully for the wedding and looked lovely—much better than the bride. Katerina wore a soft blue dress that had a V-neck and cinched at the waist; it showed her shapely figure without being overly provocative. Looking wistful with a faraway expression in her eyes, she walked somberly into the stuffy little church which smelled heavily of incense and candles burning and where most of the guests had already gathered; she walked with her head held high and her back straight as a rod, neither looking right nor left nor noticing the admiring glances of the men. Despite feeling claustrophobic, she stepped into the women's area of the church and leaned stiffly against a cement column for support and studiously regarded the numerous icons which beautified the walls as if she had never seen them in her life. She wanted to sit but the few seats were reserved for the elderly; that was probably for the best because if she sat, she might slump and demonstrate her sense of defeat, which would not be good at all. The cold metal against her back helped remind her to not lose control, especially since her only wish was to get through the day and later embrace the solitude that night could give her in her own bed. The solitude wouldn't bring peace, but it would at least allow her to suffer without having to pretend that the wrenching pain she felt in her heart and throughout her body didn't exist.

She hadn't been sleeping well and sometimes the rape scene circled through her head, over and over until her head was ready to burst and she wanted to bang it against a wall. She would find herself wanting to scream but would manage to control that and only murmur softly, "No, no, no, no." Sometimes, and just as frequently, she woke up during the night screaming and shouting, "No! No! No! You brute. Don't touch me!" In those cases, she would find her head in pain because she had already unconsciously banged it into the wall.

She was very worried that she might be carrying Giorgio's child. She should have had her menstrual period about a week after the rape. It hadn't happened and she thought that it might have not come because of the trauma she had experienced, that her body was simply protecting itself and trying to heal. But she had also missed her second period. To make it all worse, she felt nauseated in the mornings and knew from having eavesdropped on other women's conversations that nausea in the morning was a sign of pregnancy.

Katerina was worried enough that she had mentioned the lack of two periods and morning nausea to her mother three days before Michael and Ophelia's wedding day. "Mama, something's not right with my body. I haven't had my period twice in a row now and I feel sick in the morning. I hope to God that I'm not pregnant. I don't want the bastard's child. Mama, please help me," she implored.

Her mother had gotten a stricken look on her face. "Katerina," she said. "You might definitely be pregnant. After we get through this unfortunate wedding, we will sit down and look at all of this more strategically. If you don't get your next period, we will know you're pregnant and will have to decide what to do. Oh, my sweetheart, this is going to be difficult for both of us, but somehow, we will manage. My soul, my heart, my eyes, I will do everything in my power to help you."

"Oh, Mama," Katerina had responded. "What have I done to deserve this punishment? I have never willfully tried to hurt anyone. Perhaps I've shown too much vanity and am being chastised for too much pride. I've come to believe that it is my fate to never feel free and happy ever again."

Kyria Maria knew that she would not be able to console Katerina and didn't try to fake comfort. She believed Katerina's words and had sadly contemplated the same herself. This daughter might very well be lost to a fate beyond her control.

In the church, Katerina brought herself back to the present, felt the cold stone column at her back and tried to control her thoughts. She had nowhere to look but at Ophelia and Michael and she stared at them vacantly, as if in a trance, throughout the lengthy Greek Orthodox wedding ceremony. She was aware as each aspect of the traditional wedding ceremony took place but felt outside of herself, not really believing that this ceremony was truly happening. Never could she have imagined it. Never could she have foreseen it. She stared, hearing her heart first break as if an earthquake had torn it apart and then shatter into tiny little shreds that could never be put together again.

Knowing the never-changing ceremony of the Greek Orthodox Church so well, she was aware in a dream-like manner of each specific ritual as it unfolded--such as the white candles being handed to the bride and groom. She observed the exchange of the rings, the blessing of the rings, and the placing of the rings on the right hands. She heard the priest bless the stefana, the beautiful wedding crowns joined by a ribbon, in the name of the Father, and the Son, and the Holy Spirit before placing the stefana on the bride's and groom's heads. She observed the koumbaro, or bridal sponsor, who in this case was Michael's brother, step behind Ophelia and Michael and interchange the crowns on their heads three times.

Katerina distantly noted that the brother was rather clumsy in the handling of the stefana, and she had the sudden desire to giggle uproariously but managed to swallow the little burp that reached up her throat. She somewhat heard the priest's voice drone on and on in reading the Gospel, but that didn't matter because the ceremony never changed and she knew the words by heart. This very long ceremony continued with the wedding couple drinking wine from the common cup and then being led around the table. Finally, thank God, the priest concluded by removing the stefana from Ophelia and Michael and beseeching God to give them a long and joyful life with an abundance of children. First asking God for forgiveness, she intoned, "May that never happen. May your lives be short and infertile.

So that part was over. But she still had to stay for the reception—at least for a little while.

At the reception held in the church's courtyard, she greeted her sister and brother-in-law by congratulating them in a remotely polite manner and wishing them happiness. She said the right words but didn't mean them and didn't care that they knew. She couldn't touch them and couldn't look at either of them directly in the eyes, but she managed to remain poised. They didn't look at her directly either, but Michael saw enough of her to make his heart stop. She was the one he loved and had given up, he thought as he quickly reassured himself that he had made the right choice. After all, he deserved to have a bright future and had so many impending dreams for his life. In any case, it was much too late to feel regret he thought. Ophelia saw enough of her to feel a pang of sympathy, but it was her own bride's day and she wasn't about to waste energy on the little sister who had always been a thorn in her side. She had also always loved Michael and deserved him as much as Katerina. She had had to maneuver a little, or maybe a lot, to end up in this position, but, surely, she reasoned, God must have approved or she wouldn't have become Michael's wife.

As Katerina stoically turned away from the newlyweds, she bumped into Giorgo. Repulsed, she quickly stepped back and almost ran away. She hadn't expected to see him at the wedding and felt a chill sweep through her at his touch. His touch was very light this time, but she still recognized it as he steadied her from falling. His voice was low and gentle when he said, "Katerina, I'm so glad to see you looking well. I hope you will allow me to come to your house and speak with you when your mother is there. I know how badly I have misused you and I must explain myself. What I did was very wrong and I hope you will be able to forgive me."

Katerina gaped. Could this be the same man who had raped her brutally? He seemed so sincere and caring. Perhaps he was her fate after all and perhaps she was carrying his child. She didn't want to be naïve or stupid, but she had to think of the future, and, now that Michael was no longer attainable, it might be best to come terms with Giorgo. Hopefully, he was being sincere.

"Giorgo," she stated in a low, emotionless voice. "You have indeed hurt me beyond anything I can express. If you are truly the person you appear to be at the moment, you may come by. However, if you are only planning to hurt me again, please stay away. I don't know how much more my heart and soul can take."

He looked at her frankly and said, "This is who I am, and I will come to your house at the end of next week."

Chapter Four

Giorgo casually strolled down the road which led to Katerina's house the following Wednesday at 11:00 in the morning. The weather was still very pleasant and relatively warm. Usually it would have rained by this time of the year, but this year was unusual in many ways. There were a few clouds in the sky but an overall atmosphere of peacefulness pervaded the atmosphere. Giorgo always carried himself with an air of confidence, bordering on arrogance, which only enhanced his looks and added to a sense of mystery about him. He resembled his father in many ways. Tall with broad shoulders and black hair, he was a man that many women would look at twice at least. Giorgo was strong as an ox and wouldn't hesitate to take on any man who wanted to fight him. Sometimes he just wanted to fight and would start an argument at an imagined slight. His reputation for being short-tempered was well known and most men wanted little to do with him. This Wednesday he appeared unruffled and relaxed, even benevolent, as if he had no cares in the world. Bare-headed and wearing casual working clothes, he was carrying a small package in his left hand.

He greeted all those he saw respectfully and went as far as to help Katerina's next-door neighbor, a grandmother—

not Katerina's—that Katerina called Yiayia, or grandmother, out of respect and love. Yiayia was also a well-known medicinal woman and had helped birth many children. He cheerfully helped Yiayia throw hay into the barn for her donkey and tilted his head forward deferentially as he left to go and knock at Katerina's door.

"Bless you my child," Yiayia shouted after him thankfully. She was still strong but was beginning to feel her age and appreciated any amount of help she received. She thought to herself, "Maybe that Giorgo isn't really as bad as his reputation makes him out to be. Maybe his exploits or bad deeds have been exaggerated. I wonder what he is doing here and hope that it is something positive for my neighbors."

Katerina and Kyria Maria had heard the commotion next door and knew he had arrived. They had been on pins and needles since the previous Sunday wondering about the words he had spoken to Katerina and speculating about his purpose in visiting. They were appreciative and impressed by how well he had treated their elderly neighbor, as he knew they would be. Giorgo knew their customs as well as anyone and could turn on a waterfall of charm whenever it would benefit him. Acting as if out of kindness and using good manners always impressed his fellow Greeks.

"Mama, he was like a changed man," Katerina had reported. "He seemed compassionate and sorrowful, which is hard for me to accept after what happened when I was alone with him. We all know he comes from a bad family, but maybe there is more to him than we know. Maybe he deserves another chance. I hope I'm not being naïve again, but I'm really worried about my future."

"My child, let's first talk about the possibility of your being pregnant and discuss all of the alternatives. Sometimes you are very soft hearted and too quick to forgive. I don't want to overly influence you here, but we have to be thorough and very practical or we will get lost in the emotions. I want to give him every opportunity to atone for his sins against you, but I don't want to give him any occasion to hurt you more."

"First, let's say that you're not pregnant but that Giorgo wants to marry you. Would you be willing to marry him? Let's then look at your being pregnant and he wants to marry you. Would you be willing? Let's also look at your being pregnant and aborting the child. At this stage of pregnancy an abortion would be easily possible. You know that Yiayia next door has the knowledge to give you the right herbs for the child to pass through you. Of course, there will be pain with that but not beyond anything you can't bear. She would do that for you and no one would be the wiser. We both know that abortion goes against our religious teachings, but sometimes practicality must be balanced with religion."

They had started this discussion over coffee on Monday morning, lingered through the afternoon and evening and continued into Tuesday. Feeling foolish, they had even tried reading their coffee cups as if the shapes the coffee grounds made could actually predict the future. They were aware that the church frowned on this practice but were too desperate to care. They had even gone so far as to ask their neighboring Yiayia to look at their cups, but she could see nothing more definitive in the coffee cup patterns than they had. Finally, they put the cups aside and continued with their conversation as logically and analytically as they could.

Katerina kept changing her thoughts on what would be best. She wanted to make the best decision not only for herself but also for her mother. She didn't want to see her mother humiliated as the target of local gossip, and she knew that people had already started to talk and that they were not necessarily being kind. She had experienced that gossip first hand and wondered who had started the rumors.

At the well below the village, when Katerina had gone the day before to bring back water to drink and to wash clothes, she had overheard Kyria Hariklia from the village say something like, "What can you expect when a girl has no father or older brothers to keep her in line? She has had too good an opinion of herself and probably led Giorgo to the wrong conclusion. If nothing else, I know she flirted with everyone and probably flirted with him too. And the way she dances is outrageous and makes her appear ready for the sex that is condoned only in marriage! She's obviously letting the men know that she's available with or without the sacredness of marriage. The priest should probably speak with her and point out the error of her ways."

Kyria Eleni, another village woman who was having this conversation with Kyria Hariklia, nodded her head in agreement. "That girl has been spoiled by her mother. The mother has babied her and has allowed her much too much freedom. And to think that Michael from Ano Kourouni was interested enough to think of marrying her. What a fool he would have been to propose to her. We know that he could never be elected mayor with her by his side. He is better off with her sister who is sensible and modest. Ophelia is definitely the better wife for him. She will always put him before herself. I don't know if you've heard but rumor has it that she and her mother…"

When the two women caught sight of her and stopped the conversation mid-sentence, Katerina acted as if she had not overheard them. She greeted the two neighbors and went about her business as if nothing were wrong. She felt the stabs inside reverberating like knife thrusts being flicked through her, but she was not about to show them how they had drawn blood. She knew that the village had little entertainment other than the village gossip and couldn't bring herself to despise them. "Poor things, she thought. "I hope I never become like them."

They, however, feeling guilty, tried to draw her into conversation. "You probably haven't heard from Ophelia yet; after all, it's only been two days since her lovely wedding and she's probably staying inside the house with her husband as much as possible. You know how newlyweds are. I bet there will be an addition to their family within the year."

Katerina muttered an unintelligible reply and quickly finished loading her containers with water. The knife thrusts had hurt from the first conversation she had overheard, but they penetrated doubly from the questions about Ophelia and Michael. Yes, the newlyweds might well be busy starting a family.

What she had overheard told her that her mother was being criticized as much as she herself was. She forgave the two women for their words because she knew how the village people talked and observed and questioned. They were not being intentionally cruel but simply insensitive. This is how they had grown up and they were not likely to change; they wouldn't even know what to change to. She didn't approve of this aspect of village culture, but the fact was that their words mattered to her and helped her make her final decision about what to do with Giorgo and the possible child.

On Monday morning, her inclination had been that it would be best to abort the child. She had explained her position to her mother: "To abort the baby would be the cleanest way of dealing with this. It will almost be as if nothing happened. People may know some things but no one will be totally certain and they won't dare speak about this openly. Yiayia next door will not give us away and Ophelia will not speak because she won't know about the abortion. The only think that Ophelia can do is talk about the rape, but she may be afraid to do that since it may implicate her and have everyone wondering if she had some role in the assault. Besides, at this point she will be very concerned about protecting Michael and ensuring a good future. She would enjoy the life of a politician's wife and the respect that would be shown to her."

Her mother had nodded her head and said, "You make sense in what you say. It will be the cleanest option and that's what we will do if that's what you want. I totally trust Yiayia and am no longer concerned that Ophelia will put us, and herself, into a compromising position."

By Monday night Katerina had altered her view and felt it would be best to marry Giorgo. She explained her change to her mother by saying, "The church considers it a sin to willfully abort a life, and it will be difficult living with that sin since I believe what the church preaches. Furthermore, Giorgo may not be the monster that I thought he was. I tell you Mama that this past Sunday he was a different man from the one who was such a brute. I think that I should marry him whether I'm pregnant or not. Even if people don't gossip about me much, they will always have the impression that I did something wrong and no man will ever want me enough to marry me."

Again, her mother nodded her head and said, "I understand what you're saying and am only concerned about what is best for you. You know my love will always be with you and will follow you everywhere even after I'm gone. You are my heart and soul. I just want to be sure that you can trust him."

After coming back from the well on Tuesday, Katerina felt assured that Monday's decision would be the best option. She had heard the women and could imagine the rest of her life in the village as the butt of their jokes and gossip. She didn't mention the conversation to her mother because it would cause more pain and grief in her mother's heart and she didn't want to name the women because they were supposedly friends with her mother. Katerina merely repeated what she had stated the previous day and felt a level of relief that she had not had for some time. Her decision was made, she would wait for Giorgo to arrive, and they would go forward.

They heard his knock and immediately opened the door to invite him into their small, sparsely furnished living room which basically had a fireplace, a wooden table, a small couch and two chairs. The cots her brothers slept on had been folded and stored in the bedroom. Thinking of her brothers, Katerina was glad that they were too young to understand what was going. On the walls hung beautiful blankets that Kyria Maria had woven on the loom as part of her dowry years before. These bright blankets were multi-colored with geometric designs repeated over and over. On the fireplace mantel stood a portrait of Katerina's father from many years earlier. He had been a kind man that she remembered fondly and often missed. He had been such a reasonable person and never raised his hand or spanked her in anger. The few times he had smacked her bottom had been more difficult for him than for her, and he had done it more out of the need to show her guidance than to truly discipline her. This is what he had said and she believed him because he had explained to her the responsibilities of being a parent and his sorrow in having to spank her with a couple of swats.

At their invitation, Giorgo entered the room and sat in one of the chairs. He took out his little package of sweets and handed them to Kyria Maria asking her to please accept a small gift for allowing him the chance to perhaps redeem himself in their eyes.

Katerina made them some coffee and poured it into the small, demitasse cups. As they slowly sipped, Giorgo asked permission to begin: "Kyria Maria and Katerina, I have come to explain myself today and hope that you will listen to me with open minds. I must have been crazy to have treated her as I did and I only want to make amends."

They nodded their heads and he continued: "Kyria Maria, I would like to marry Katerina. She may not want to marry me after my atrocious behavior. I don't even know how to comprehend, much less explain, what I did. I'm not looking to make excuses for myself, but I truly don't understand how I was capable of such stupidity, arrogance, and violence. Please, please forgive me, or, if that's not possible, please allow me to show you I'm not the vulgar monster you believe I am. I must be a very weak man to have lost total control of myself and hurt Katerina so intensely. Perhaps it's because of my great love and attraction, but, again, I can't use those feelings as excuses and I know that love is not expressed through rape."

Kyria Maria studied him carefully, looking for something—anything—malevolent in his nature, and said in a serious tone, "The decision has to be Katerina's. She is the one who felt your actions first-hand, she's the one who has suffered directly, and she is the one who needs to forgive you. I will let her speak."

Katerina rose, looked at both of them frankly and said very simply, "I have put much thought into this decision. I believe that people can make colossal mistakes for a variety of wrong reasons and wrong circumstances, and I believe in practicing the charity of forgiveness. I do forgive you Giorgo and hope we can make a life together. I don't think the man you were the other night is the man who truly lives in your body and soul. That man is not who I now see in front of me. Giorgo, I will marry you and be a good wife to you and a good daughter-in-law to your parents. I hope that we may have children and a good family life."

Chapter Five

The wedding ceremony took place two Sundays later on October 26, 1919, immediately following the church liturgy. It was late morning and there was more than a hint of fall in the air. The day was clear but somewhat crisp, and there was a contemplative feeling in the church. Everyone had a somber appearance, including the usually jovial priest, and the space echoed with unvoiced protests floating in the thick air. Were the saints in the icons brooding? Did the Virgin Mary look distressed? What was this melancholy that had settled over everyone? This was an ancient service that they all loved to watch and usually were joyous in the knowledge that it had been celebrated for centuries. This was a service full of love and symbolism demonstrating the ideas of a positive marriage and focusing on love, respect, equality and sacrifice for each other.

Unlike Ophelia's and Michael's wedding, there were few people in attendance. Few had been invited and few would have wanted to attend. There were about twenty in all and most of them would have preferred to be elsewhere. There was the immediate family standing in the appropriate and opposing sides for men and women and a couple of very close neighbors like Yiayia who lived next door. The neighbors had fondly watched Katerina grow up, and they stood at her wedding with a prayer for her happiness in their hearts. And they made their crosses continually and reverently.

The wedding service began at the entrance of the church. The church was located above the village in a wide enough area for local festivals and large gatherings. The road to and from Kato Kourouni was situated directly to the side of the church, which made it a convenient spot for those who were from other villages. Father Kosta, dressed in the long priestly garments that touched the ground, began the ceremony in the traditional manner by asking Giorgo and Katerina if they had come of their own free will and were not promised to someone else. They responded affirmatively that they had come of their free will and that they had not promised themselves to anyone else. Their affirmations then allowed Father Kosta to invite them and their attendants to enter the church and walk to the altar.

Giorgo was dressed formally in a dark suit which showed off his rugged body and handsome face. He looked very calm and self-assured as if he had the future carefully planned. No sign of stress showed on his face or in his eyes. Although obviously subdued, he regarded everyone with an expression of inner peace and patience. His calm expression hadn't altered much even when Katerina met him outside the church; it may have deepened into something resembling self-satisfaction and possessiveness, but only a careful observer would have noticed.

Katerina also looked very calm and moved slowly in a trance-like state toward the altar once Father Kosta invited them into the church. Her eyes were hypnotically expressionless like still water in a deep well. The guests couldn't help but wonder about her thoughts, but they didn't really want to know. Father Kosta felt a tinge of concern when he looked at her but felt powerless to do anything more than continue with the ceremony. Even he, however, noticed how exceptional she looked.

Her beautiful black hair was arranged around her face in a twisted French pleat and her green eyes were startlingly large. She wore no make-up other than a little powder and a touch of lipstick. Her dress was light pink, long-sleeved with the V-neck style she preferred. It was belted at the waist and fell just below the knee. She wore a nice dark low heel an inch high but no nylon stockings since they couldn't afford luxuries. She had taken extra care with her bath the night before and still had a glow from having scrubbed herself so thoroughly. Katerina also had put on her best underwear—never-worn underwear that she had sewn in the last year in anticipation of her wedding night. Of course, when she had sewn the underwear, she had been dreaming of Michael and how it would feel to be kissed by him, to be touched by him, to lay with him and have him teach her what it meant to make love.

She saw Michael and Ophelia out of the corner of her eye but refused to look squarely in their direction. Without really studying them, she couldn't help but notice the they did not fit as a couple, he being tall and slender and she short and plump. How silly that somehow, she had expected their marital state to transform their looks into a more harmonious state. But Ophelia looked happy enough so, obviously, Michael had given her the marital experiences and pleasures that should have been Katerina's.

"Do not go there," Katerina said to herself. "Their happiness or unhappiness has nothing to do with you. You cannot allow yourself to become bitter. If he has come to love her, you can't stop that. And even if you could, what would you gain? Nothing. It's too late to think of what might have been."

Having walked to the Altar and standing to the left of Giorgo, as required, she faced the priest resignedly with a straight back. She vaguely heard him bless the rings in the Betrothal, the first half of the service, and slightly felt him placing her ring in her right hand. Slightly again, she felt their koumbaro, their sponsor, exchange the rings between her and Giorgo three times to signify that their lives would be entwined forever.

Father Kosta then blessed the stefana, the wedding crowns, and made the sign of the cross three times. He read from the Bible—an epistle from St. Paul—urging them as husband and wife to work toward unqualified love and assistance of each other.

Giorgo and Katerina drank wine from the common cup, signifying that they would be sharing the happiness and sorrows of life together. They were to be forever intertwined within the Church's teachings and within their existence on earth; all earthly and unearthly sensations, tangible rewards and disappointments were to be shared equally and compassionately with each other. The biblical phrase that accompanied drinking from the common cup was pronounced:

I shall partake in the Cup of Salvation, and I shall invoke the name of the Lord.

Father Kosta then led them around the wedding table three times, with the Bible in his hand, to remind them that the Word of God should lead them through life, with the circle around the table representing eternal marriage with no beginning or end. The two being united in marriage would be forever connected. While walking around the table counterclockwise in the "Dance of Isaiah," the priest chanted:

Rejoice, O Isaiah! The Virgin is with child,
And shall bear a son Emmanuel,
Both God and Man,
And Orient is His Name,
Whom magnifying we call, the Virgin blessed.
O Holy Martyrs,
Who fought the good fight and have received your crowns,
Entreat ye the Lord,
That He will have mercy on our souls.
Glory to Thee, O Christ our God,
The Apostles boast,
The Martyrs Joy,
Whose preaching was the Consubstantial Trinity.

Father Kosta, after the long but traditional ceremony that had been established centuries before, finished with his heartfelt blessing that they may be fruitful with many children to provide joy and happiness, companionship, and love. Hearing Father Kosta talk of children, she felt relieved that she had not gone through with the abortion. It would have been a great sin to destroy the little life growing inside her. She, who had a hard time hurting or killing anything, would never have been able to forgive herself for destroying her own flesh and blood.

"My baby," she whispered in her mind. "I will love you and protect you to the best of my ability and more. I only hope to give you as much love as my own mother and father have given me. Oh, my sweetheart, I can't wait to see you. You will be so beautiful! I don't care if you're a boy or a girl. I just want to hold you and nurse you and smell you and have you by my side. I love you already so much! We'll play games and take walks and come back to naps, and… and…we'll have fun."

After the wedding ceremony, Katerina forced herself to stop daydreaming because she had a role to perform and needed to treat her guests properly; she had always been a polite and considerate person and didn't want anyone to feel slighted. So, she was determined to make everyone feel special when the group went to Kyria Maria's house after the wedding ceremony.

At their house, several tables had been laid out in the small courtyard. The tables were covered with Kyria Maria's fanciest cloths and had a small bouquet of roses in the middle. It was not a fancy gathering, but Kyria Maria and the female guests had prepared plentiful food and sweets, which they served along with the home-made wine brought out especially for the celebration. It was so beautiful, so thoughtful and creative that it tugged at Katerina to cry with joy and appreciation. She didn't cry then knowing that she would do so later with her mother and friends. Her gratitude to them would last forever for making her day extra special and for making her feel so well loved.

Kyria Maria, as hostess and mother of the bride, warmly welcomed the guests to her home: "I am very thankful to each of you for joining us today in honor of Katerina and Giorgo. May all of you, and all of your relatives, have good health and much happiness in the years to come. Let's all now salute the newlyweds and wish them a wonderful future. Salute!" She raised her glass.

Everyone raised and clinked their glasses to acknowledge the new couple, and the celebratory afternoon continued with more food and more wine and congratulatory speeches. "What a wonderful festive gathering this was," everyone said as they left.

Having had enough drink to loosen their tongues, a few said, "There was an odd feeling at the church that made us uncomfortable at first, but it was obviously some type of strange phenomena. Bless you and the children and may you have health and happiness forever."

It was late when the party finished and Katerina and Giorgo were able to leave. He had been gentle and attentive to her all evening, and he was awfully handsome she thought. With a little romance on his part, her heart might move from Michael to Giorgo. Why not?

She looked forward to something special with him in their future. Over time, meaning since Ophelia and Michael had married, she had forced herself to put prior dreams behind her and closed off her feelings about Michael. She had refused to concede to mental images of Michael and Ophelia sexually coupling and, not knowing what was real anymore, she had refused to accept, or was suspicious of, the supposed reality around her. Maybe her sister and brother-in-law were happy, maybe not.

Looking at the wedding guests in the small yard, Katerina felt so much affection toward most of them. She wanted to kiss them with love and gratitude and friendship—other than Giorgo's parents that she didn't know well and sensed only coldness directed toward her. She would show them respect but doubted she would ever feel fondness and warmth for either of them. They were a good-looking couple but very standoffish as if they considered themselves a step above everyone else. Perhaps they had set their sights on a daughter-in-law who came from a wealthier family and would bring a large dowry with her. Probably, she thought, they would never be satisfied with any woman that their son chose. She would just have to deal with it.

Toward the end of the reception, the encouraging speeches and strong wine had lulled Katerina into a soft and sleepy mood; after all, this was her wedding day and she had the right to be a little tipsy. She was so glad that they would not have to walk to Ano Kourouni. A cousin had loaned them the use of his donkey and cart and they were going to ride to their residence. The few articles that Katerina still had at home were placed in the cart and, at Giorgo's command, the donkey carefully stepped forward.

She saw the house they were to live in within fifteen minutes. Riding in the cart was so much quicker than walking. Most of her belongings had been taken there the previous week and had been put away properly. As part of her dowry, she had numerous blankets, tablecloths, kitchen items, and all that was needed to open a new home. She had cleaned the house thoroughly and decorated the rooms with bright blankets over the sofa and the bed. Oh, how she looked forward to being responsible for her own home! She would take care of it with love and imbue it with her happy spirit so that it would always be a welcome refuge to her children. They would laugh and sing and dance within those walls.

On the negative side, Giorgo's parents would be living with them, but that was customary and Katerina didn't have any problems with it. At least they weren't totally within the same structure and each couple would have some privacy from the other. The parents would have the first floor and Katerina and Giorgo were to live on the second. The house was simple and spotless with all of the basics of the time, and Katerina felt no concern that it was not finer in style or space. She had never had very much and was grateful for what Giorgo could provide. In reality, it was much nicer than the home in which she had grown up.

Together they climbed the stairs and entered the front door. The stairs here had a balustrade that she thankfully held on to since she was still just a little tipsy. The porch at the top was also wider than that at her mother's house and she was glad that it would be so much safer for their children. They heard nothing from downstairs and assumed the parents were already asleep since they had left the party a couple of hours earlier. They placed the few items in their hands on the floor in the living room and proceeded to the bedroom where Giorgo quickly stripped Katerina of her clothes and underwear. She had planned to put on a special gown which was made specifically for her wedding night but she understood that he wanted her right then.

Still, she felt some alarm and said breathlessly, "Giorgo, please be kind to me. Remember what we promised each in our wedding vows. We are now united in marriage and should support each other. I am now your wife and will always fulfill my marital obligations, but please be gentle and not hurt me as you did before."

"You want kindness and dare reproach me for what happened before?" he retorted with a suddenly angry and raw voice. "I have wanted you for years and pledged to have you regularly even if marriage was the only way. I have no desire to be kind and gentle. As my wife, you will have no choice but to follow my commands. I am the man of this house. Lean over the bed now so that I can take you from behind and don't pretend you don't like it. This will be a wedding night we will both remember. I have played your game long enough and now you're going to play mine." He then pushed her and she fell onto her stomach on the bed.

"Giorgo," she cried, mortified by what she had just heard. "You told me that this is not your nature. You've apologized to me for what happened before. I believed you and thought we might be able to have a decent life together. I hurt so much before. Please don't act this way."

"You bitch! You've embarrassed me in both villages. Everyone knows you and your mother went to ask Michael to marry you. You had no shame. I see how you still look at him and how he looks at you. He may want you, but I will be the one with my penis inside you as often as I want. I am master of this house, and I will do as I please with my wife. I may have some further plans for you and you will not say no to me."

He excited himself with his words and hardened even more. "Yes!" he congratulated himself. This is how it should be."

Not paying attention to her cries of pain, he thrust himself inside of her. She cried non-stop as she felt her rectum tear. "God, my God," she moaned. How can you let this happen to me? Why are you making me suffer so much? Your Son suffered and died for the world, but I don't think his pain could have been worse than mine."

Giorgo finally relieved himself in her and withdrew. He gazed at her without any remorse and said, "Do you now understand? You will do as I say and you will have sex with me as often as I want. You are now my wife and my possession. Go wash yourself."

Katerina stumbled to her feet and found a basin with water and a cloth. Very gingerly she pressed the wet cloth against her rectum and almost fainted when she saw the blood. It was dark in the room but there was enough light that she could make out the bloody imprint. She had brought medicinal supplies with her in one of the bags and she searched for some salve to apply. She found the salve, and, again very gingerly, applied a small amount with her finger

The first attack a couple of months previously had hurt and shocked her. This time was even worse because she had believed him when he claimed to be ashamed of himself. He had appeared so sincere that she had agreed to marry him. He must think of her as an idiot. What he thought didn't matter, but what he could do and what he planned to do mattered very much. Dazed, she wondered if he planned to kill her. That he might kill her didn't matter either. Finishing her off might be the most merciful thing he could do.

Chapter Six

The sun was just starting to emerge as Katerina struggled out of bed. Unlike the day before, the view she saw through the small window didn't show any promise of sunshine. In fact, the sky looked downright gloomy and menacing. She hadn't slept at all during the night thinking of how she would be able to escape this time. Giorgo had slumbered off almost immediately after his tirade and she had heard him snoring throughout the night. She was thankful for that since he wouldn't be bothering her while asleep.

It was amazing how at her slight movements he instantly woke up and watched her intently. "You must be getting up to make me breakfast I take it. I can't imagine that you would have anything else in mind, now would you? You're probably hoping for a repeat of last night." he goaded her.

She felt disgusted and scared to see how he was lustfully staring at her naked body and merely said, "I can make you breakfast if that's what you want."

"Yes, I want breakfast but I want something else before that," he gloated as he reached for her. "I want to enjoy my property to the fullest."

She tried to resist but knew her efforts were useless. Without further words he shoved her on her back and immediately entered her. He thrust into her repeatedly while she softly cried. She hurt so much but knew that begging him to consider her pain would only make him hurt her more. The more she cried, the more aggressive he became as if he took joy from her grief.

"You know, you might as well start enjoying this and start giving me the appropriate responses that a wife owes her husband. You should start by taking my penis into your mouth and massaging this gift I have for you. I see you shaking your head, so I guess I need to show you how. This way you'll know what I like and you can start the lovemaking by sucking me in the future."

Over and over he forced her to submit to him without any tenderness on his part. He only had tough words for her and a great desire to dominate. Blood was splattered throughout the sheets as if sprinkled generously from a healthy supply. Some of the blood was dry but it was obvious that not all of the blood had been distributed at the same time, indicating that the abuse had been sustained over an extended period. Giorgo had kept her in the bed for several days and only took breaks to eat or wash. He only laughed when she suggested that they leave the house for a short while, as if he understood very clearly that she would use the opportunity to escape.

"Why would we leave our love nest? Everyone knows that newlyweds need time to adjust to each other and to enjoy each other in bed," was his usual retort.

He also started taunting her about paying her own way in the marriage. "You can't expect me to feed and clothe you without any contribution from you. We need money and you need to bring in your share. The paltry sum that your mother gave for your dowry will not last us long."

Katerina couldn't understand where he was headed with those types of comments. Her dowry was not rich but it had been decent—as decent as Ophelia's and Ophelia had not mentioned that Michael was complaining about the size of the dowry. "Why are you saying these things?" she questioned. "Ophelia and I have equal dowries and Michael has not complained about this."

"Of course, Michael hasn't complained," he shouted angrily, obviously wanting to hit her. "Ophelia knows how to treat him well as her husband. She is a woman who understands how to treat a man. She doesn't expect him to provide without giving him everything he wants."

But it quickly became clear where he was headed when he brought one of his old buddies to the house later that day and introduced him to Katerina. He had made her clean herself and the bed before he left and told her that she had better behave properly and entertain any guests he brought back with him. Upon his return, Giorgo casually explained to her that she would now have the opportunity to ensure that she would be paying for her portion of expenses. All she had to do would be to have sex with the friend and the friend would pay Giorgo handsomely.

She was aghast! He had hurt her, assaulted her, insulted her in every way possible, and now expected her to become a whore. "No!" she shouted to him. "I am not a whore and I will not allow you to sell me. This is too much and I will make that very clear to your friend. I doubt there is a man who would pay for me knowing what I feel." He caught that this was the wrong time to push and decided it would be best to leave well enough alone for now. He could always intimidate her later—especially if he punished her a little bit.

While he was careful to in no way bruise her face, he took no care with her body. He used it fiercely in whatever way suited him. He was a savage, a brute, a misogynist and had no shame about it. Deep down, he took pride in what he saw as his manliness.

By Thursday morning, only several days after her wedding, she knew that her body could no longer handle the mistreatment. Katerina felt terribly sick and tried to sit down. She would have loved a cup of tea but didn't have the energy to boil water. She realized why she was feeling so sick and what was happening to her body when she looked at her legs. Blood was seeping out of her vagina in a steady stream and, suddenly, something besides blood landed on the floor—something more substantial. It had to be her baby.

"He has killed the child that I promised to love and protect. That villain who is the devil's spawn has destroyed innocence one more time. May he suffer! May he die in thirst! May he die with worms eating his heart! May he die with ants biting his penis! May he die! May he die!" she shrieked while she shook violently.

She found a towel and tried to gather the formless shape that was an unrecognizable blob. Katerina clutched the towel to her breast, moaned, and let the tears fall. She vowed to dig a hole and bury her dead baby in a secret place that he would never find.

Giorgo found her on the floor rocking back and forth with the towel. He saw the blood still oozing from her legs and the red towel and realized something serious had occurred. A flicker of fear went through his mind as he wondered if the local police might come after him, but he wasn't afraid of the one local yokel who basically patrolled the fields. But, if not the police, perhaps neighbors would be outraged and come to Katerina's defense. Everyone knew that she had no one to stand up for her and they might decide to act as a vigilante group.

"How ridiculous that would be," he said out loud. "I have done nothing wrong in my house and if my wife accuses me of anything, I will deny any of her allegations."

Katerina had heard him come in and only said, "You need to bring my mother and Yiayia here. If I keep bleeding like this I will die." She didn't ask him to bring his mother. The woman must have heard her screams on multiple occasions but hadn't come to check on her even one time. He didn't suggest bringing his mother either since he knew she didn't care enough to be concerned.

He left frowning and somewhat disconcerted and returned with Kyria Maria and Yiayia impatiently on his heels within the hour. Yiayia, having helped with many births realized instantly what had happened. "Let's get her into bed and wash her," she told Katerina's mother. "We will need to cut strips of cloth to stem the bleeding and we will need the herbs I've brought. Hopefully, the herbs I will apply and the herbal drinks I'll make will save her. She has miscarried and may not be able to become pregnant again. For now, we will do well if we can at least keep her alive."

Kyria Maria trembled as she looked at Katerina and fell to her knees with a keening sound as if already in mourning for her daughter. She clutched at her stomach and brought her head forward to the ground and wailed. The sounds were heart wrenching in their intensity and pain. They were the sounds of a mother feeling gutted with unspeakable loss and wanting to die.

Yiayia, having no alternative than to take charge, slapped Kyria Maria to contain any further hysterics and said sternly, "Maria, get up and help me now! If you don't, your daughter will be in her grave before you. Do as I say and we will save her."

Yiayia continued coldly as she looked directly at Giorgo, "You, you bastard, have apparently been the cause of this. You're an arrogant donkey who doesn't have the brains of a flea. May that big-headed penis that you are so fond of cause you to be afflicted with the plague in your groin and gonorrhea, syphilis, or chlamydia on itself, and may it fall off after you suffer. If I were you, I'd start praying that she lives. When people hear of this, you may not be so lucky."

Chapter Seven

It was touch and go for a week whether Katerina would live or not. She moaned continuously and thrashed around the bed. Sometimes she could be heard whimpering, "No, please don't. Please, please don't. I hurt so much. Mother help me. God help me." She had a fever up to 104 degrees at times and the priest came to see her daily. Father Kosta was ready to give her the last rites as practiced by Greek Orthodox Christians, which included partaking in Confession, Holy Communion, and Holy Unction since she was close to death, but he held off when he felt her unconsciously shrinking from his touch. He knew the fever was consuming her, but he also sensed a struggle of the spirit pulling away from all that she had ever believed in.

Father Kosta was there when she ranted bitterly at God, "You may be out there somewhere, but you haven't been here for me. I have no faith in you. You are no longer my God! I have no God! You, like others, have betrayed me. Worse, you deserted me in my hours of need. You saw and did nothing to help me. You do not deserve to be called God!"

He understood her anger and only held her hand while she raged. He could only hope that something positive would emerge from the hatred she now felt, and he prayed to God for empathy toward this poor, lost young woman who had gone through an inferno no one should ever experience. He prayed deeply after she knocked the chalice of bread and wine out of his hands when he tried to give her communion as part of the last rites. "Please, Father in heaven, forgive this poor child for her act. She has always been devoted to You and is now rejecting you out of pain. I know that she has always loved you and has tried to act with the same compassion You showed in sacrificing your Son. She truly does not know what she is saying right now."

Kyra Maria and Yiayia stayed by her side constantly, murmuring softly, singing lullabies as if to a child, and not leaving her alone for even a minute. They had developed a routine and adjusted their shifts whenever one of the two appeared overly tired. They washed her caringly, with as light of a touch as possible, and tended to her wounds carefully. Yiayia had brought the herbal medicine, the proper salve, the mountain tea, and her love. She made fresh tea as often as necessary and, supporting the limp body caressingly, made sure that Katerina would sip some of the brew on an hourly basis.

The first day, Yiayia had cut away the vaginal hair as much as she could so that she could apply salve more easily to that area. She was trying to ward off any further infection and mixed the salve with herbs to make a concoction of extra -healing properties that she had learned from her own grandmother and mother. It deeply wounded her to look at that area and know how bad the injuries were, but the evidence was clearly there and she scathingly swore at

Giorgo. She was only a local medicinal woman, but she had had enough experience with childbirth and physical trauma to see how extensive the damage was; the cuts, the ridges in the skin, the blue and black bruising, and the ugly swelling told it all.

Yiayia hadn't wanted to let Katerina's mother help at first. She didn't want the mother to see the story unmistakably evident on Katerina's stomach and vaginal area. So, she did as much as she could to make Katerina presentable before accepting Kyria Maria's help. And, she realized, she had done the right thing when she heard Kyria Maria gasp at the sight of her daughter's injuries.

"The devil himself couldn't have done more," Kyria Maria whispered in shock. "May he die for what he has done. No, forgive me God, but may he live and feel the same torture for what he has done. May the bastard be brought to his knees and face death with no compassion from anyone. I will not let him near her again and am willing to die to make sure he never again touches my child."

"Yes," Yiayia agreed with a deep sadness. "He is a brutal man. We had heard terrible rumors about his family, and, from what I see here, they must have taught him this sadistic trade very comprehensively. May their stay in hell be eternal. His mother and father live downstairs and must have heard something, but they must not have been willing to intercede on Katerina's behalf. Hopefully, they didn't endorse or promote what happened here."

Disgusted with the marks they could see on Katerina's body, the two women decided to gather Giorgo's clothes and packed them in a box. They placed the box outside on the little porch and wrote, "Do not enter this sad and grief-stricken house. You are not welcome! Suffer, you bastard, suffer!"

When Giorgo returned to the house after having had some ouzo with his buddies in the kafenio, he agilely went up the stairs to enter what he considered his bastion. He saw the box on the porch and read the note in shock. Anger started to rise in him from his toes and snaked to his head, and he could barely control himself. "Who do these two old women think they are? How dare they tell me what to do in my own domain? I am the master of this house and I have done nothing wrong," he reassured himself.

He stepped forward to open the door and found it locked. Fury consumed him in a flash and he kicked at the door, shouting, "This is my house and you will stay here only if I allow it. You two old bitches, open this door. Now!"

Yiayia opened the door and stood there impassively. "You may not enter. You are not welcome and this is no longer your house even though it is legally in your name. You will need to change that as soon as possible. Morally, it is no longer yours and we can't allow you to defile the space here any longer. We cannot allow you near Katerina since she is teetering between life and death and your presence may impact her enough to drive her over the cliff into oblivion."

He swore at her: "Old lady, do not tempt me to do you harm. You are in my way and I will do what I have the right to do. Move aside!"

"If this is what you want, I will move aside for now, Yiayia muttered as she backed away from the doorway.

He stepped into the room and realized that a figure was standing in front of Katerina's bed. It was Kyria Maria and she held a pistol in her right hand that was pointed directly at him. He found it grimly humorous that she had the audacity to confront him with a pistol. He doubted that she barely knew how to load the gun. These two old women thought they were pretty tough.

"I will die before I let you go any further," she warned him. "You will stay out of this poor house and you will stay away from my Katerina. I will not hesitate to kill you now or later, and, if you think you can remove me from this matter by causing my death first, I will have written instructions to the villagers about how they need to follow up with you, and I will explicitly detail what they should do to you so that no one repeats your vile acts. You mongrel!"

She continued: "You may not believe me and you may not be familiar with how well I can use this gun. Take one step further and I will demonstrate my expertise. Katerina does not have a father to protect her and her brothers are still children and cannot come to her rescue. But, take my warning now and leave quietly and immediately."

Of course, he didn't believe her resolve to kill him if necessary or her expertise with a gun. He had only seen the motherly and nurturing side of her nature. Stupidly, he took that step forward, and before he actually put his foot down, she had aimed at and blown off his big right toe.

He screamed in pain as she laughed: "Another move and I will take off your left toe. I'd like to make sure that your feet are a matching pair. Feel the pain and know what is in store for you."

He was in pain, but, with a quick spin, he was out the door and down the steps, clutching at the railing so as not to fall forehead. He saw the blood seeping through his shoe but was scared enough to not sense how badly it hurt. His goal was to get into his parents' house as quickly as possible and have one of them tend to his wound.

Yiayia and Kyria Maria clutched each other at the sign of his retreating back. They hugged tightly in relief and affection and snickered: "Katerina, if you were only awake enough to see how that obnoxiously mean buffoon reacted to a small threat. The coward! May he be damned forever and may all his toes fall off. Better yet, we'd like the pleasure of blowing them off slowly one by one!"

Katerina merely moaned softly, but it seemed that she had comprehended, at some level, what had taken place. She would continue to battle the fever for about a week, but for these moments, an aura of peacefulness surrounded her.

The fever was mighty and had Katerina burning through her skin, through the bed, through anything that touched her other than the cool cloths and the cool hands with which they tended her. She dreamt but had no idea what was taking place. Sometimes the dreams were nightmares but sometimes the dreams had a gentleness to them. She saw her father as if she were again a child and then a young teenager. The pride and love he felt for her shone through his eyes, and his touch on her was very sweet.

"My Katerina, stay with your mother," he gently murmured. "I love you and her and eventually we will all be together, but it's not time for you to come now. I want you to live and to feel joy, and I want you to be there to comfort your mother as she will be there to comfort you. My child, I couldn't help you, and I felt such grief because I could see what was happening. Please forgive me. If only I could have been there to protect and shield you from beasts like Giorgo, but I was taken too soon. I can't tell you why God allows monstrosities like Giorgo to exist, but I still have faith. I know you have lost yours for now, but I also know that we have a merciful and forgiving God. I can't be there physically to touch or comfort you, but feel my breath against your cheek and know how much love I feel. Do not die yet."

She felt his breath of love and made her decision. She would live but as a changed person.

Chapter Eight

The fever broke the following Thursday, one week after Katerina's mother and Yiayia had arrived to tend to her. They had urged her to drink liquids as much as possible and to sleep. They sponged her through the sweating bouts she went through and covered her when they saw her shivering and trembling. They knew she was generally very weak and simply held her hands or massaged her forehead and temples to relieve the headaches she seemed be feeling. They recognized when she was hallucinating and they knew that she was confused. They heard her talking in her dreams and felt her convulsions when she was having a nightmare.

After the fever broke, Katerina was still very weak but she was lucid. Day by day, her strength improved until one day several weeks later she said, "Mama, I have been able to stand for the last two weeks and am feeling strong in body and spirit. I will need to settle my affairs with Giorgo sometime soon. He will never fool me again, and it is I who has the upper hand this time."

Her mother had been expecting this and merely said, "Yes, I know. Do you want us here when you confront him?"

"No, I need to do this myself, but, don't worry, I no longer fear him. I feel in control of myself and the situation and my future. If you could, however, I would like for you to leave the pistol here with me. I don't plan to shoot him, but I do want the gun available and in a safe place."

"All right, Katerina, when you are ready for him, let us know and we will leave you alone for the day. Yiayia and I can then go out and pick some fresh greens from the fields for dinner. Horta is one of your favorite dishes and it will give that extra iron that you need in your diet."

Katerina knew that she was ready to confront Giorgo a few days later. Her mother and Yiayia pampered her that morning by brushing her hair and making a special breakfast of soft-boiled eggs, cheese, and bread for her. She drank some herbal tea and milk to wash down the food, and she felt strength flow throughout her body.

Kyria Maria went downstairs, knocked on his family's door, and nearly spit at his mother when she answered the knock. "I'm here to ask Giorgo to go upstairs and talk with Katerina," she said."She is ready to discuss matters with him. Is he here?"

Giorgo's mother knew better than to invite her in and simply nodded: "Yes, he is here. Let me ask him if he can go upstairs now."

She returned and, without uttering even one word of apology, let Kyria Maria know that he would be upstairs within the hour, to which Kyria Maria nodded and went to let Katerina know. Katerina acknowledged the message and asked to be left alone while she waited for him. Within the hour, there was a knock on her door and she shouted, "Please enter."

He hadn't seen her since he had been run off by her mother and Yiayia, and he was amazed at how good she looked, especially since she had almost died several weeks earlier. He began with, "Katerina, my wife, let me begin by going on my knees to beg your forgiveness. There must be a sickness in my brain that causes me to do harm to those I care for most. I so regret having hurt you again, and I hope you didn't take me seriously about having sex with my friend. That was merely a foolish attempt to joke. It was more than foolish. It was stupid, stupid, stupid."

She appraised him coolly and retorted: "This is no time for silly words and useless explanations. You and I both know what you are, and I can no longer be misled by your idiotic, melodramatic acts. I am telling you to not even try those games on me because it will only make the penalty worse for you."

"Oh, "he thought to himself. "So, you think you are the wily one now. After the number of times that I have duped you, you now think you can outsmart me. You're just a woman and if you think you can match wits with me, you're very mistaken." And he had the gall to not hide the little smirk on his lips.

She saw the smirk and read his thoughts correctly and gave him a negligible but ironic smile that he didn't even catch. "I know what you're thinking. I can see into you and I will let you know that you are playing a dangerous game. I am no longer the mild and naïve Katerina. I have certain powers and am aware that I can hurt you greatly. Sit down and let me tell you what I have planned."

Somewhat surprised at her unresponsiveness to what he had considered a magnanimous, even apologetic, gesture to their conversation and eventual reunion, he sat on one of the chairs. She gestured authoritatively for him to move to a chair at the table and told him she had papers that he would need to sign. "Papers?" he wondered. "What could she be thinking of?"

She also sat and they faced each other across the table before she began a lengthy discourse: "I plan to stay married to you and to live in this house. However, you will not live here with me but will stay downstairs with your parents. We will not touch physically again, but you may visit and do whatever you want with as many other women as you please. I'm not interested in that aspect of your life. You will turn the house over to me legally, and you will not have a key to the door. Additionally, you will provide me weekly with enough money to survive and some extra change for minor items I may need from time to time."

"What are you talking about?" he asked in bewilderment. He was totally taken aback and stated, "I have no plans to go along with anything that you have said. Why would I? You seem to have forgotten who is the man in this house, and I will not stand for such language any longer."

"You will do as I say because the length of your life depends on it. I will continue with my instructions so that you may have a clearer picture of what I'm talking about," she answered solemnly. "Now, you have no choice in the matter because I have cursed you to hell and have given you up to one year to live. You are aware, but have probably forgotten, that I have some special powers passed to me by my paternal grandmother. I have never been interested in developing those powers because of my faith in God. The time has come, however, that I need those powers and I will use them to the utmost. You think of women and me as powerless, but you will learn differently and regret that you ever met me."

Dumbfounded, he stared at her but didn't say a word.

She took a sip of water and went on, "My grandmother, or so the story goes, had the power to place curses. She didn't truly believe that she had that power, but the time came when her curiosity demanded that she explore the possibility. One day, in anger, she swore at her neighbor Kyria Marianthi and wished her to have the worst year of her life. In fact, that's exactly what happened to Kyria Marianthi that year: she lost her husband, had sick animals, and broke her ankle. Of course, my grandmother felt guilty when she saw her neighbor going through a terrible period and refused to even consider ever placing a curse on anyone else. Besides, my grandmother was a religious woman and didn't want to offend God. After all, we know that placing a curse is the devil's work and the consequences of such actions can be disastrous.

"I know you've heard rumors of this story before, and I know you believe in this power. You've done the devil's work enough to grasp evil. So, I'm now telling you that I've placed a curse on you to die within one year. Today is November 28, 1919, and you have until November 28, 2020 at the most. I can't lengthen the period for you to live, but I can shorten it. I can also choose how you die and how much you will suffer in this death. Therefore, I'm giving you the ability to negotiate. Unlike God, I'm willing to bargain.

"I have had a contract written up. Here it is on the table. Please read it now and sign it if you want. If you prefer to think about it for a couple of days, that's fine also. I will expect to see you two days from now at the same time. Now, please let yourself out."

Chapter Nine

Giorgo was terrified. He recognized that he was going to die but didn't want to believe in the inevitable. "No, Giorgo, don't listen to her wild statements about curses. Maybe her grandmother did have some powers, but that doesn't mean that Katerina does. Yea, yea, we've all heard rumors about her grandmother but that's all they ever were—rumors!" he fiercely whispered in an attempt to reassure himself. But, deep down, he felt the fear nibbling in his stomach and knew that he was going to die. He knew that he would have only a year at the most to live.

"God damn her!" he shouted with additional expletives streaming out of his mouth. "The witch has cursed me and there's nothing I can do to change her curse."

Absentmindedly he delayed descending the stairs and just sat for some minutes. He finally entered their door and managed to terrify them just by the look on his face. They were anxiously awaiting his return to hear about his visit with Katerina. Knowing what a smooth talker their son was, they had expected him to enter triumphantly. This defeated man was not the son they had expected to see.

He told them haltingly, "She has put a curse on me and has given me one year at the most to live, but she might decide to shorten that time period if she chooses. She can even decide how I will die and the amount of pain I might suffer. She wants the house turned over into her name, wants to stay married, but to have nothing to do with me. How can this be? This is not the woman I married. Mother, father, what am I to do?" They also understood the power of the curse that select people had and they knew that Katerina and her grandmother belonged in that fold.

"Well," his mother responded in an appalled voice, "this is not the woman you married but this is a woman who has the power to do with you as she pleases. I don't like this at all but I don't see any choice other than to go along with her wishes. Maybe we can all talk with her, promise her whatever she wants, give her whatever she wants, and find a way to remove this curse. She says she can't change what she has already pronounced, but I don't believe that is true. I've heard of similar cases where the curse has been successfully removed. The witch! The bitch! My poor son that you ever got involved with someone of her kind."

His father wasn't so cool in his appraisal: "Let me go upstairs and strangle her now," he shouted. "Let me go and put my hands around that white, smooth throat and slowly squeeze the life out of her, the ungrateful whore! She has been given a house to live in and has been supported by us. What has she contributed? Nothing! All she has done is complain that her husband has shown too much love and longing for her. Instead of being appreciative that her husband desires her, she had made him out to be a monster who beats her. The ungrateful whore!"

"Now, now," Giorgo's mother interjected much more calmly. "Yes, you could kill her but that will only ensure that Giorgo will have one year only. I understand that these witches have power even after death, and I don't think we should challenge that power at this time. Let's do better with this or we will lose our son."

Giorgo was pleased to hear that there might be a possibility of removing the curse. He knew it would be difficult to change Katerina's mind, but he was too young to die and willing to give her whatever was necessary in exchange for his life. Did he really care about the house? No, not really. Would he be willing to support her financially? Yes. He and his parents weren't rich but they weren't poor. If he only had a year left, the money would be useless to him.

But dammit, she was blackmailing him. That whore!

"Stay levelheaded," he repeated over and over inwardly. "She has you in a straightjacket and the only thing you can do is go along with what she wants. Do as she says and you might survive. You can still have women and that's about the only thing that means much to you anyway. She said she doesn't care how many women you have and you know that's true. You won't be able to remarry and have children, but you've never wanted children, so there's no loss there. Besides, you no longer desire that blackmailing bitch from hell."

"Mother, you're right," he murmured agreeably. "Under these circumstances, we need to placate her and give her what she wants. She will live upstairs so we will see her occasionally, but all we must do when we see her is to greet her politely and let her pass by. I will sign the house over to her immediately and give her a weekly stipend."

He continued in a resigned voice: "We need to talk with her and discover any chance to change what appears so fatefully written at this moment."

His mother replied somberly, "Yes. I have heard that if the curse is removed, another curse can never be applied to the same person or anyone close to him. Yours and our safety rests on that curse being removed. We will lose the house but perhaps the Church could find a way to absolve your marriage and allow you to remarry. In our religion that is almost impossible, but we can always try."

"We'll have to check with Father Kosta first. He can give us guidance on how to proceed. That the marriage has not been in effect for more than a year will be to our favor," Giorgo's father said broodingly. "I doubt that Katerina cares if you're divorced or not. She just wants to make you pay for whatever sick acts she's imagined and that's why she wants the house. That woman has mental problems and the priest is bound to recognize that. I'm sure Father Kosta will intercede for us and help us to change her mind about this curse. Placing a curse on someone goes against all teachings of the Church and is considered colluding with the devil, which will lead to damnation for her soul and eternal life."

His mother added, "I believe that Father Kosta will say that with prayer, fasting, faith and Holy Communion, the curse she has placed can be conquered and destroyed of any power. Before we go talk with Katerina, let's first say a prayer and go to the church to light candles and talk with Father Kosta. We may not have always done the proper things in our lives and now need to follow our religion more faithfully."

Chapter Ten

In the months since he had married Ophelia, Michael had had various revelations including that the marriage had been a tragic mistake. But it was too late to undue the marriage vows and divorce was not an option. He cursed himself for being the weak fool that he had been in turning down Katerina, and he blushed at how callously he had treated her. The look of disbelief and disappointment on her face that day she and her mother came to visit him would haunt him forever. He had thought only of his promising future and hadn't realized how bleak that future would appear without Katerina by his side. The fault was not with Ophelia but with him. Ophelia loved him deeply and was happy to do anything he wanted, but he couldn't reciprocate those emotions no matter how hard he tried.

"Michael, my sweet husband," she would coax him many evenings. "Let me give you a massage to take away any pain you're feeling. You've worked hard in the fields today and your back must be aching."

She would massage him and invariably rub his loins and penis slowly until she felt him harden. She wanted him to make love with her regularly and had found that this was the easiest way to excite him. She feared that he didn't really want her and that he dreamt of Katerina while he was inside her. She was totally correct in her deduction but hoped to win him over by seducing him regularly.

"Come Michael. Make love with me. Do whatever you want. My body is yours as is my heart and soul."

Being a young male with healthy and strong erotic instincts, Michael responded sexually as she surmised that he would. He had her as often as three times a night and sometimes when he came in from the fields at lunchtime. It seemed he couldn't fulfill his sexual appetite even though it was with the wrong woman—maybe because it was with the wrong woman. For Ophelia, however, every time he entered her, she felt victorious over her sister.

Ophelia bragged to herself often: "So little sister, he is mine now. You wanted him but I'm the one who has him. Maybe he doesn't love me yet, but he will over time. I give him my body and we bond as husband and wife. That is something you will never have!"

He made love with Ophelia, or in his mind had sex with her, but he wanted to shout out Katerina's name each time he released himself. He would close his eyes at that moment and picture Katerina below him or above him or to the side of him or in front of him, depending on the position he and Ophelia were in.

He would picture Katerina's beautiful creamy face, her large green eyes, her sculpted lips, her luscious long throat, her black hair, and her soft, curvy limbs. "Dear God," he would find himself praying after every sexual bout with Ophelia. "Will I ever stop seeing her in my mind? Every time I mate with Ophelia, I betray her by thinking of her sister. I want Katerina! I want her and her only! What I'm experiencing is not healthy and I know it. If I could change it somehow, I would. It's too late to change the marriage but there must be a better way of coping. After all, this is going to last my lifetime. God help me, I don't know what to do and I have no one to whom I can turn."

One winter morning in early January, he thought of his friend Niko and decided that Niko would be a good and wise confidante. Niko was fifty-one years old and had experienced many things in his life, some exciting and some heartbreaking. He had left the village and worked on the ships for many years, so he had traveled worldwide. He had gone to the Americas, Australia, Russia, and various ports in the Mediterranean.

Niko had started his sea journeys at the young age of twenty. He had signed up as a seaman because there were no lucrative jobs in Ano Kourouni or in the area, and his family didn't have much land to farm. He had been struck by a young woman a couple of years younger than himself and had spoken to her family before leaving on his first journey. He had gone to her father and explained that he would like to marry the daughter when he returned from America—the first journey. He stated that he had spoken to the captain and the captain had reassured him that they would be back within one year. Niko explained to the father that he didn't want to marry Aphrodite, the daughter, until he returned because he had so little to offer her in the present. However, after the first voyage he would receive a healthy sum of money to be able to support Aphrodite and even to buy a little land to farm.

Aphrodite's father had observed Niko for some time and was aware of the flirtation between Niko and his daughter. He thought highly of Niko because Niko was hard working and ambitious and so obviously infatuated with Aphrodite. He approved of the marriage but also thought it wise to wait until Niko returned.

"Niko, my boy," he said and thumped Niko enthusiastically on his back. "I have known for some time that you and Aphrodite have been eyeing each other. I know that she will be happy to marry you and I am glad because I care for my child's happiness. We have a small dowry to give her but nothing to brag of. As you know, we are not rich, but we are proud and hold our heads up anywhere we go. We will welcome you into our family as we know your family will welcome Aphrodite. Go now knowing that Aphrodite will be yours in one year. Please come back to visit with the family and Aphrodite before you leave."

Niko did indeed go to visit and the upcoming marriage was formalized in an engagement celebration. Aphrodite and Niko couldn't keep their eyes off each other and blushed throughout the dinner when they were often caught staring in love and anticipation. They were allowed to kiss each other's cheeks before Niko left, but that was all. They would have to survive on romantic dreams during the absence.

Although the captain had promised that Niko would return in one year, it didn't happen that way. The ship's owner insisted that they take another vessel in America and drop off wheat in South America. The captain literally had no choice but to agree to do so. After all, his livelihood and the livelihood of his seamen depended on being available to do whatever the owner wanted.

So, they travelled to Brazil in South America and put in another year's time. Niko had written Aphrodite's father to explain the situation and felt comfortable that the father and Aphrodite understood and wouldn't think he was trying to stall the marriage. He loved her so much and dreamt of her regularly, often waking up hard and sweaty.

From Brazil, the owner sent them with another load to Russia. That was a difficult journey and another year passed. Niko was becoming frantic that he would never be able to return to Ano Kourouni again. He thought about what Aphrodite and her family must be thinking and how worried they must be about her getting up in marriageable age. Yes, they knew he was sincere and that he loved her, but that couldn't help them if he didn't return and marry Aphrodite.

He finally did return but four years had passed and when he returned, Aphrodite was married to another man from the area who was probably the wealthiest farmer around. She appeared to be happy and already had one child. Niko was stunned upon discovering this. A sadness enveloped him that never totally left him over the years. Sure, he laughed and danced. Certainly, he eventually married a good woman from a nearby village and they had a compatible relationship and several children. He had nothing to complain about and thanked God for his health, his good wife, and his children. He never complained, but thoughts of the lost opportunity to marry his one and only true love sneaked into his mind daily. He often wondered if the quest for money had been worth the price.

This was the man that Michael wanted to talk with. This was a good man who had lived honorably in his life despite disappointments and frustrations. Michael, as everyone else, knew his story and had always admired him for placing his family first and providing for them with a giving and generous heart.

Michael found Niko in the kafenio drinking coffee that wintry January afternoon that bleakly belied the return of summer and the warming rays of the sun. There was less to do on the farms in the winter and the men would invariably gather in the kafenio to exchange gossip or ideas on how to improve their farming techniques. Michael joined Niko's table and talked amiably for about an hour with minor chitchat before turning to Niko to ask him if they could talk privately at another time.

"So, my young friend, you want to speak with me on a one-to-one. I sense that you have some deep issues bothering you. Of course, we can talk and, if I can help you with something, it would please me greatly. Obviously, you have confidence that I will never repeat anything you say or you wouldn't be requesting this. Let's meet tomorrow afternoon at my house. My wife and children will have left to visit her sister in Kymi and we'll have all the privacy we need."

"Thank you so much my friend,' Michael nodded thoughtfully. "I knew you wouldn't let me down, and yes, I have all the confidence in the world in you."

The following afternoon, Michael stopped by Niko's house before going back to his own. He had told Ophelia, although he felt terrible about lying to her, that he would be talking with Niko about possibly buying some sheep from him and that he might be a few hours late. As he expected, she had no problem with that and lovingly told him that she would hold off dinner. She also rubbed her breasts against him and said, "After dinner, there might be a very special dessert awaiting you. I'm sure that you'll be interested in a unique delicacy that I can offer you." That didn't surprise him either.

Michael and Niko sipped small glasses of red wine while they talked. Everyone annually stomped the few grapes they harvested each fall and stored the juice in barrels downstairs where the animals were boarded. The soil in this area was too poor and rocky to produce many grapes, so the wine was especially treasured. This wine had aged well over a couple of years and had just a hint of retsina in it. Mm, it was so tasty and the retsina gave it that unforgettable tang that would instantly make one think of Greece.

"Niko," Michael started when all the pleasantries had been dispensed with and it seemed appropriate to begin the serious discussion. "I have made a great mistake in marrying Ophelia, and the fault is all mine. I didn't love her before marrying her and don't love her now. I'm going crazy having sex with her and thinking about Katerina the whole time. Sometimes I feel so guilty that I don't know what to do. I don't want to live with this hypocrisy all my life, but I don't know how, or if, I can change my emotions."

Now, now," Niko countered. "There is never a situation where it is only one person's fault, but I understand that is how you feel. Tell me more."

"I should have married Katerina but didn't feel at the time that it would be the right thing for me to do. I had ambitious notions of going into local politics and running for mayor. I even thought that, if I became mayor, I would have the opportunity later to look at a higher political position in the area. I'm sure you've heard what happened to Katerina with Giorgo. No one talks about it but everyone knows. I was simply too cowardly to marry her because of the ramifications that scandal would have on my goals."

With a sad twist to his mouth, Michael continued: "She and her mother came to speak with me after Giorgo raped Katerina, and they asked me to marry her. I, thinking only of myself and stupidly wanting a virgin, refused. I foolishly felt that people might not see me as a serious enough person to become mayor if I married a woman with the reputation of having previously had a sexual encounter. Of course, it wasn't her fault but her reputation was damaged. And to top it off, I was afraid that she might be carrying Giorgo's child. I just couldn't accept that.

"Now though, I am with a woman I don't love. We have sex more than often enough, but I feel nothing other than general affection for her. She knows how to arouse me in many skillful ways and does that to make sure I won't stray. But I have no feelings of love for her. I'm not even very attracted to her physically even though my actions may appear differently to her. She does not attract me like Katerina still does. Ophelia is a good woman but her face has little appeal and her body is too fleshy and thick. How am I to live with this marriage the rest of my life? I don't blame Ophelia. I only blame myself, but that doesn't help me resolve anything and I do want a resolution."

"And you have come to me because you know I have had some bad luck in my love life. You know what happened with Aphrodite years ago. You must be looking for some help in surviving your marriage and building a stable future. After all, the church teachings won't allow you to commit suicide or get a divorce," Niko said slowly and carefully to make sure that he wouldn't offend Michael by being presumptuous in summing up the situation.

"Yes, you are exactly right," Michael agreed sadly. "I know that life has not given you what you hoped for, but you've managed to deal with that. Please, tell me how you have survived."

"First, I think you must truly accept the finality of what has happened in your life. I think you have but are suffering because you also accept your own stupidity and responsibility for the decisions you made. I was incredibly sad when I heard of your impending marriage to Ophelia instead of Katerina," Niko said shaking his head forlornly. "I wanted to come to you and strongly urge you not to make a monumental mistake, not to make a mistake with long-term consequences. I should have come to you, but I was fearful that I would be seen as a prying and gossipy old man and that I would offend you.

"I'm now going to tell you that no man or woman will be able to offer you proper advice, but I will talk about my friend Dr. Petro Makropoulos who lives in Halkida and works at the hospital there. He also made a fiasco of his life. On the surface, he appears well-balanced and satisfied, but he knows what he did and the mistakes he made. He suffers but accepts his fate. I'm going to tell you his story because it is sadder than yours. It may not help you, but you'll know that we all have our sorrows to bear and yours may not seem as profound relative to his."

"All right Niko. Tell me anything that might help me, anything to help me accept my fate."

"My friend Petro was a brilliant man and studied medicine here in Greece. He stood out from other academics and received a scholarship to conduct special research in internal medicine at Weill Cornell Medical College in New York City, New York. Cornell is a prestigious institution, founded in 1898, and Petro was greatly honored at this opportunity. Of course, he jumped at the offer and went to New York.

"He didn't have a great deal of money, so he rented a room in a nearby boarding house which offered both breakfast and dinner. The owners and managers, Roberto and Maria Ortega, had arrived as newlyweds from Puerto Rico approximately thirty years earlier and had a daughter, Elena, who was twenty-four years old. She was a lovely young woman who had gone to college and worked in the banking sector. Of course, she lived at home and helped her parents with the lodging business as much as she could. She had become friends with a couple of other young women in the boarding house and was happy to have their company."

Michael remained quiet and occasionally nodded as Niko relayed the story of Petro Makropoulos and Elena Ortega. These are the words that Petro as conveyed to me: "Elena was absolutely lovely. She was a small and dainty thing but very strong with slender limbs that moved gracefully. She had brown curly hair that fell to her shoulders and clear blue eyes that teasingly observed the world. Her lips were somewhat average until she smiled; but, her smile lit up the room and was irresistible once it was directed at you.

"Petro was immediately attracted to her, but she didn't respond the same to him. It wasn't that she didn't find him attractive. She did. He was quite good looking, with a body resembling that of a soccer player. He was muscular and dark with typical Mediterranean olive-skin and black, laughing eyes that could so easily charm women. He knew the effect he had on women and didn't hesitate to take advantage whenever he could. He felt no guilt about taking advantage since his philosophy was that everyone had free will and the women who slept with him did so because of their free will. Besides, women in America were known to be much looser than women in Greece. and he couldn't be blamed for their actions."

"So, Dr. Petro Makropoulos was quite a player?" Michael asked.

"Yes, my boy, Petro was quite a player and proud of it. He was not one to give up easily on a woman who presented a challenge. Elena was a challenge and, because of that, she increasingly became more desirable to him. He started wooing her cautiously so as not to scare her off. After a couple of months, she agreed to go out with him. She didn't want to develop emotions for him and became concerned when she realized that, indeed, she was beginning to care for him deeply. She had heard about Greeks, their volatile nature, possessiveness, and macho attitudes toward women. The last thing she wanted was to have a relationship with a Greek. She knew it would be impossible to continue a long-term relationship and a dalliance with him could lead to nothing permanent.

"However, she continued to see him daily at the boarding house and went out with him more and more often as time passed. As you would expect, her heart became tangled and could no longer hold out against him. They were at the heavy kissing and touching stage when one of her girlfriends at the house told her to be careful with Petro." Elena did not appreciate this and became defensive.

"Why are you warning me about Petro?" Elena asked her friend huffily. "He treats me very well and I think he's becoming serious about me. I didn't think there could be any chance of an enduring connection, but I'm now wondering. Marriage has crossed my mind since he told me that he loves me. He was so romantic and serious when he said it that my heart skipped or opened or whatever it does when you fall in love."

"Elena," her friend responded seriously. "I'm warning you because when he sat between us the other day on the little couch in his room, he tried to fondle my breast. I don't know what he was doing to you, but he did touch me. Of course, he made sure that you couldn't see any of this. I should have slapped him right then and there but I froze. He has a reputation as a womanizer and a womanizer doesn't change. There's a reason for the saying 'old dogs cannot learn new tricks.' He may truly love you, but he's a womanizer and you know it."

Niko took a pause to shake his head and continued by describing how devastated Elena felt and that she confronted Petro immediately. She needed to know the truth! Petro vehemently and angrily refuted what Elena's friend had said. He claimed that she had tried to flirt with him and was basically jealous of Elena. Not knowing what to believe, Elena decided that her friend had been speaking out of jealousy and was deeply disappointed. They had been such close friends—basically roommates living in the same house together. She felt sorry for her friend but wasn't about to give Petro up on a trumped-up charge. After all, he had said he loved her and continued saying so.

"The friend," Niko recounted, "felt she wouldn't be able to help Elena and unhappily moved out at the end of the month. Elena purposely lost touch with her and gladly put the incident and the warning out of her mind.

"I shouldn't be telling you such private details, but I know this will go no further and Petro was very descriptive about their relationship. He knew that she was feeling closer and closer to him, thrilled to see him, to touch him, to hear him, to be near him. Her heart was full of love, and she joined him in his adjoining room one night. She went to him freely out of love and wasn't disappointed. He was quite experienced, and she was a virgin who was very willing to let him teach her what to do and how to please him; he, in turn, was happy to please her, to touch her everywhere, to kiss her, to lick her, and to slowly and patiently enter her. Sometimes he was wild with her and thrust quickly and desperately, but she enjoyed it as much as he did. Of course, he knew how to protect them from pregnancy and she trusted him in that.

"Elena was so happy and she now could envision a life with Petro comfortably—at least that's what she told him. Sure, there were differences in their cultures, but those differences could be overcome. Still, she knew that her parents would not approve of what was happening under their roof and was very careful to keep her love affair with Petro a secret.

"She was in this unbelievably happy state until the day she overheard talk from Petro's room. How unusual, she thought. He must have a female relative visiting. She had come home during the middle of the day as she wasn't feeling well and was lying in bed when she heard Petro's voice and another, a feminine voice, talking and laughing. She thought that she should probably join them and meet this relative, but she just wasn't feeling up to it. Nevertheless, wondering what was going on and not wanting to feel left out, she went and listened at the bedroom wall that they shared. It was then that she heard the bed creak and the voices change from conversation to moans and sighs. Of course, she recognized what was taking place next door and threw some clothes on in order to go and confront Petro.

"I'll be there in a minute," he shouted frantically when she knocked at the door and shouted his name. He had been caught. "I'll be right there Elena. I just need to use the bathroom first.

"He went to the door just a bit disheveled but with a smile on his face. "What's wrong Elena? You're not usually here at this time. Are you sick?

"Yes, I'm here because I wasn't feeling well at work. I heard some commotion in your room as if you had a female visitor here and want to know what's going on.

"You're right. A friend of a long-ago friend happened to be visiting New York City and decided to look me up. She came by to catch up on old times and we had a wonderful conversation about the past. You probably just heard us laughing and talking. She was just about to leave when you knocked on the door.

"At that, a somewhat tousled and unattractive woman joined Petro at the door and quickly pecked his cheek goodbye before brushing by Elena. She hadn't looked Elena in the face as if embarrassed by something or other.

"Come in my sweet Elena," he invited. "I'm so sorry to see you not well my love. Maybe if we cuddle a little, that will help you.

"Elena, feeling and acting very suspicious, walked into the room. She saw that the bed had quickly been made and smelled the aroma of sex. "You had sex with that woman," she accused him. "How could you? You've said you love me many times now and we've even talked about marriage. She wasn't even appealing with that pock-marked skin and heavy body. How could you? Don't you even care who you have sex with? Are all women just a vagina to you? Am I another vagina to you?

"Petro, seeing how upset she was, thought it would be best to take a walk out in the air. He definitely didn't want to stay in the room that even he could tell smelled of the sexual encounter. He suggested the walk to her and they roamed around the block for an hour. He wanted to hold her hand but she maintained a distance between as if she didn't want to be touched. Sensing her distraught state of mind, he swore, "I did not have sex with her. I don't even find her attractive. I didn't touch her." He claimed this over and over. "I swear on my mother's grave that I am telling you the truth. There is nothing more sacred that I can swear upon and you must believe me. Please Elena, don't do this. Let's go and have coffee and talk about our future seriously. Let's talk of marriage. Let's talk about first visiting Greece to see if you could imagine living there.

"They walked into a neighborhood coffee shop and took a little booth in the back as far away from other customers as possible. Elena didn't believe him, but she loved him and allowed herself to be persuaded that she had misheard and misinterpreted what had taken place in his room. He repeatedly spoke of his love for her and she succumbed to his charm and expressions.

"Let's visit Greece this summer," he suggested. "I'll take you to my family's house so that you can meet all of the relatives. They will welcome you and be happy for us. I'll find someone to teach you Greek in the meantime, and that should make you more comfortable there. You know I love you and that you're the only one for me.

"She agreed to the plan and they went to speak to her parents once they returned to the house. Her parents weren't pleased, but they didn't want to stand in the way of their daughter's happiness, so they agreed to the trip and the future marriage.

"That summer Petro and Elena arrived in Greece. The trip across the Atlantic took about two weeks. The ocean was relatively calm and the trip was smooth. After arriving in Piraeus, Petro took her to see the sights in Athens, and she was awed by the Acropolis, the Temple of Olympian Zeus, the Plaka, and Cape Sounion. She especially enjoyed the nightlife during the two days there. They then went to visit his family in the port town of Kymi on the eastern side of Evia on the Aegean. She loved the town, and his family welcomed her warmly. She had no complaints of them.

"He, on the other hand, seemed to be testing her persistently. Often, he seemed very remote and at times was sexually aggressive. Although they had sex once at the family home when his family went to visit friends, it was in fact more of a rape. Technically it couldn't be considered a rape, but it had that feeling to her because she knew that he would have insisted on sex whether she agreed or not. That incident made her feel very lonely and question how he would treat her in Greece. What if they married and he treated her poorly? Would she be able to escape? She would be under his control with no family nearby to turn to. She felt apprehensive and he offered no comfort.

"He discerned her thoughts and became angry that she would question anything about Greece, no matter how reasonable her trepidation might be for a twenty-four-year-old foreigner. The day after the supposed sex, he disdainfully told her, "You don't think you'll be happy here, I can tell. If you're not going to be able to adjust, I don't want to marry you. I need a wife who will support me in everything and who will stand by me during my career. I will have a prominent position here and need a woman who will help advance that career. I can't have a woman who might hold me back.

"She understood and agreed that marriage might not be the best thing after all. He appeared a changed man in Greece and she felt frightened by the ups and downs in his personality. He seemed so domineering in Greece and she was scared that she would never be able to question his behavior; the society and culture were so patriarchal and men did pretty much as they pleased. She was further aware that the men often womanized but that women would be condemned for that same conduct. And, she clearly remembered the incident her friend had referred to about him touching her breast and the episode in his room with the long-ago friend who had stopped by to see him.

"Yes, Petro, I'm scared of what life here might be for me. I love you so much and want to be your wife, but you are probably right.

"Hearing her agreement, his heart and mind hardened against her. He had brought her here and now she was rejecting him. Well, she wasn't really rejecting him since he had rejected her first, but the fact that she questioned their future together in Greece infuriated him. If that was how she was going to be, he didn't need her. She certainly hadn't passed the test this visit had provided. In any case, he would eventually return to his country and find the proper woman to marry and develop his career.

"They left by ship again after a two-week stay. They were on amiable if cool terms, but they still made love and were attached to each other. The primary difference was that they now recognized they would not have a life together.

"After arriving in New York City, they decided it would be best if Petro moved elsewhere. They agreed to not see each other again, which didn't last long. Every so often they would again agree to not see each, but the separations never lasted. Consequently, loving each other while knowing that they were courting heartache, they remained as a couple for the following two years. She knew he often saw other women and hurt every time she found direct evidence of his involvements. Sometimes she found condoms in his new quarters, but he denied all her accusations. Sometimes she found women's underwear, but he couldn't understand how the underwear had gotten into his laundry or insisted that it was hers and she was just being unreasonable.

"What a fool she was to stay with him. But she was a fool and stayed, and as the time approached for him to return to Greece she felt fear. He hadn't broached the topic of marriage again, and she hadn't either because of her stubborn pride. She was also afraid that his answer would be an unequivocal no. They had an agreement that he would return home without her. The night he left brought her whole-hearted misery and made her glad that she had kept a bit of her pride and hadn't pleaded with him to reconsider.

"He had told her in late afternoon that he was going to go around and say good-bye to friends and that he would stop by to see her after that. She waited and waited, watching the hours tick by on the clock, in the boarding house living room and finally fell asleep on the couch. At 2:00 AM, she was awakened by a soft knock at the door. How little he must think of me she thought. This was his last evening here and he didn't care enough to spend it with me. The hell with him! His actions tell me more than I want to know. So many years together and this is how it ends. The bastard!

"She walked to the door but didn't open it. Instead, she walked to the window next to the door and opened it so that she could speak through the screen. "You have shamed me by your actions unnecessarily. Not even on your last evening did you bother to show me respect. I may not mean much to you, but I have loved you like no other. I don't want you to touch me now. Go to hell! Go to hell and burn!

"Of course, he left," Niko said slowly as he drew to his conclusion. "Petro had no choice at that point. At some level, he was relieved to not have to spend his last hours with a sad and tearful Elena. He came to his beloved Greece, gained a prominent position, married a suitable woman for his lifestyle, and had three children. He thought of Elena every day, and, rumor has it, that he lights a candle in her name every time he enters a church. He was successful and gained everything tangible that he had worked for, but Elena haunted him in his dreams. The choices he had made had seemed so correct at one point. Had they been the best choices? If they had been, why was he still thinking of her with a wrench in his belly?"

"You were right," Michael acknowledged. "This story is worse than mine, if for no other reason than that he had years to come to his senses. All I can conclude is that he didn't truly love her enough or he would have acted differently—both in New York and in Greece. I feel for Elena and want to know what happened to her."

"I don't really know and hope that she found someone to love her that she could love back. The one and only thing that Petro has told me about her after he left is that she wrote him a letter several months after his departure. She told him that she had had an abortion. Her mother had taken her somewhere where they performed this procedure. It was a painful ordeal but she thought she had no other choice."

Although Niko hadn't been able to actively advise him, Michael felt more at peace as he walked home. He had made the decision to marry Ophelia although it was the wrong thing to do. He knew and accepted his responsibility. He had rejected Katerina unfairly and deserved any disgust she felt for him. He would live with Ophelia until one of them died. They would have children. He would simply have to learn to live with Katerina lingering in his mind and heart.

Chapter Eleven

Giorgo, his mother, and his father went to see Father Kosta and told him what had occurred between Giorgo and Katerina. Having baptized and known Katerina all her life, Father Kosta was aghast and highly distressed to hear that she had purposefully and specifically cursed Giorgo. Father Kosta had been apprised of Katerina's grandmother's powers, but he knew that she had been a religious woman and chose not to use her abilities destructively. He also knew that the granddaughter was like her grandmother and would never hurt anyone intentionally. He looked at the little group sadly and said: "This is not the Katerina that I know. She has always been devout and strong in her religious beliefs. I cannot imagine what brought this on, but I will talk with her and find out."

"Of course, Father, talk with her, but please tell us what we need to do to remove this curse. Please guide us. We are God's repentant servants and want to act accordingly"

"What we are talking about here is "Vaskania," or the evil eye. It is an ancient term and originally meant envy but now also refers to maligning, denigrating, slandering, using harmful power and doing general harm. We know from our religious teachings that every evil that happens comes from the devil and not from God. 'We know that 'Every good gift and every perfect gift is from above, coming down from the Father of lights' (Ja. 1:17).

"Additionally, we realize that 'Bless and do not curse' (Rom. 12:14) tells us that the spirit of evil comes strictly from the devil. St. Basil the Great wrote a treatise titled 'Concerning Envy and Vaskania,' and he also wrote exorcisms that we will use with other prayers in our battle against the devil.

"You have done the right thing to turn to the Church. I will bless you with the cross, which will help to protect you; the cross, you know, has great power against evil spirits. Wear the cross always! Be sure to not wear special charms because that would be promoting magic and paganism. Do not be tempted by any other 'exorcism' for this will show your lack of faith and impiety toward God.

"You need to understand," Father Kostas continued, "that for the Church to effectively fight evil, you must truly express your faith through your daily actions. You must implement and follow God's commandments in your lives. More specifically, you must go to Church regularly, pray fervently, confess and take communion. With prayer, we communicate with God. With confession, we are absolved from our sins which are a burden upon our soul and a wall that prevents God's grace from sanctifying and protecting us. With Holy Communion, we are united with God Himself and we become 'gods by grace.' We must also use the rest: the sign of the Cross, prayers and exorcisms by me or another priest. So be careful and avoid every non-ecclesiastical means of sanctification."

Father Kosta saw the look of confusion or perhaps frustration on their faces and felt he had to explain further. This family had never been active in the Church and didn't comprehend what was expected of them. He knew he needed to be as clear as possible: "There exists only one special prayer for Vaskania which is found in the ecclesiastical book, Small Euchologian; a book exclusively for priests. Only one who has the grace of the priesthood, who has participated in the Mystery of Ordination, is allowed to deliver such commands in God's name and such supplications to God on behalf of the praying Church. It must be clear that these prayers are said only by priests."

The three nodded in agreement and Father Kosta intoned, "Let us pray to the Lord…Lord have mercy." He solemnly recited the prayer against Vaskania, against the 'Evil Eye':

Lord our God, Sovereign of the ages, almighty and all-powerful, creating all things and altering them merely by willing it: the flame in the furnace of Babylon, heated sevenfold, you turned into dew, preserving the three youths in safety. Physician and healer of our souls, safe haven for those who hope in You, to You we pray and You we entreat: drive away from Your servant Giorgo, expel and banish every sinister action, every satanic assault and plot, the wicked and harmful meddling by mischievous, wicked people casting envious eyes.

Whether it was beauty or gallantry or good fortune that provoked malice and jealousy, ill will and an envious eye, loving Master, extend Your mighty hand and raise high Your strong arm; consider this Your creature as You watch over him, and send him an Angel of peace, stalwart guardian of soul and body: to rebuke and repel every wicked intent, every spell, and the grudging looks of hurtful and envious people.

Thus, guarded by You, may Your suppliant sing to You in thanksgiving: "I have hoped in God:

I will not fear what men could do to me." And again: "I shall fear no evil, for You are with me.

For You are "Mighty God, Wonderful Counselor, everlasting Father, Prince of Peace. Lord our God, be gracious to Your servant Giorgo and spare him any hurt or affront by the eye of malice; safeguard him above all through the intercessions of our most blessed and glorious Lady, the Theotokos and ever-virgin Mary, of the luminous Archangels and of all Your Saints. Amen.

Father Kosta continued with the 'Prayers of Exorcism for Those Assailed by the Spirit of Evil and for All Afflictions':

Let us pray to the Lord. Lord, have mercy.

God of Gods and Lord of Lords, creator of the flaming ranks and maker of the bodiless Powers, You have crafted all that is in heaven and on earth, yet no man has seen You nor can; the whole universe trembles in awe before You.

You once throttled the Chief of the Fallen Angels when out of disobedience he breached his proper function; You dashed him to the earth along with his rebellious angels, who then became demons, and hurled them into the depths of darkness.

Make this exorcism, performed in Your dread name, strike fear in him, the leader in wickedness, and in all his ranks, cast out with him from the light above, and put him to commanding him and his demons to retreat completely from Your servant Giorgo and from this house, that he may work no against those sealed with Your image. Rather may they who have been so anointed with power find strength to tread upon the asp and the viper and all the power of the enemy.

For Your most holy name, of the Father and of the Son and of the Holy Spirit, is praised and magnified and is glorified in awe by everything that breathes, now and always and forever and ever. Amen.

Father Kosta finished with the last prayer, the 'Prayer of our Father among the Saints John Chrysostom Archbishop of Constantinople':

Let us pray to the Lord. Lord, have mercy.

Everlasting God, who delivered humankind from bondage to the Evil One, free this Your servant Giorgo from every action of unclean spirits. Command these evil and impure spirits and demons to withdraw from the soul and body of Your servant Giorgo and not to hide in and dwell in him.

In Your holy name, and that of Your only-begotten Son and of Your Holy Spirit, let them be driven out of the work of Your hands, so that free of every satanic assault, he may live a holy, righteous and devout life, deserving of the sacred Mysteries of Your only-begotten Son and our God, with Whom You are blessed and glorified, together with Your all-holy, good and life-giving Spirit, now and always and forever and ever. Amen.

The three departed after profusely thanking Father Kosta for the prayers he had recited. They solemnly swore to him that they would be in church regularly, pray daily, wear the cross, go to confession and take communion. They pledged that they were going to turn their lives around and become good Christians to the point of financially helping some of their more unfortunate fellow villagers.

"We are now going to talk with Katerina," they informed him. "We will go to her and ask for her forgiveness for anything and everything we have done wrong. We will turn the house over to her and provide her with enough money to live moderately. We would like to give her more, but we plan to take on some of the financial burdens of our neighbors who have had bad luck with their crops this year."

"Bless you and walk with God in your hearts. I will also go to see Katerina this afternoon."

They talked with Katerina. She was by no means warm toward them and barely let them into the house. She looked well and healthy physically, but her face no longer had a sweetness to it and her mouth was set in a grim line. Her eyes were determined and fierce as if expecting to fight. She offered them no refreshment and didn't ask them to be seated. They were obviously not welcome.

"What have you come to tell me?" she demanded.

"We have come to apologize and ask your forgiveness for anything and everything we may have done to hurt you," Giorgo's mother said softly.

The father added, "We are here to let you know that we will turn the house over to you and provide you with living expenses. We will stay out of your way and don't expect even a 'good day' from you. Be assured that we will never trouble you again. We went to Father Kosta and emerged as different people after talking with him. We have seen the error of our ways and plan to be good and true Christians in all our actions from this day forward."

"Giorgo, what do you have to say?" she queried.

"I am in total agreement with everything my mother and father just said. I hope you can forgive me. That I will never bother you again I swear in God's name! I am not saying this because of the curse you placed on me but because I have seen the error of my ways. God help me to become a good and changed man! Father Kosta prayed and lifted the curse, so I'm not doing what you want out of fear but out of desire to transform my life"

Katerina regarded him without expression. "I have no forgiveness left in me. Your life is your own and I need know nothing about it. Although I will be living close to you and might occasionally see you, my desire is to never see your face again. However, I know that is impossible and simply accept it as part of my daily chore. I've now heard enough and want you to go. We have nothing further to discuss."

Shortly after they left she had a visit from Father Kosta. "My dear child, what is all this that I hear? Giorgo and your in-laws came to see me and told me that you had placed a curse on him. Of course, I instructed them how to conduct their lives and prayed to lift the curse from him. I have faith that they will now become true Christians.

"My concern, however, is no longer about them but about you. You have always been a sweet creature unwilling to hurt anyone. What has happened to alter you so much and to allow you to so dangerously associate with the devil? The devil is at the bottom of all curses and you, Katerina, know that very well."

Although she no longer had faith in the Church, she still respected Father Kosta enough to feel compelled to give an explanation of what had occurred between Ophelia and herself and Giorgo and herself. She stoically and thoroughly went over all the details and saw tears in the priest's eyes. Naturally, being a village priest, he had heard quite a bit of the local gossip about the horrible turn her life had taken, but he hadn't heard the gritty, almost unbelievable facts. His heart ached for her.

"My child, you should have come to me. I baptized you and have known you all your life. You are like my own daughter and I would have done everything in my power to help you, both as a man and as a priest. How much your dear mother must have also suffered! Please don't turn away from the Church now. I know that it is hard to maintain your faith with all you've experienced, but it is critical that you keep your faith in God. He is the only one who can save you. Do not have anything to do with the devil for that will lead to your destruction. Let us pray. Would you pray with me now?

"No Father, I no longer pray. I have lost my soul, my way, and my heart. I no longer care that I am a wretched creature. I will live my days sorrowfully and accept that as my lot for the rest of my life."

"My child, my child. Don't despair. Just know that I will always be here to help you when you are ready to accept help. God's house and compassion are open to you."

Very distressed, he left her and went back to the Church to pray for her soul.

Chapter Twelve

Katerina knew Ophelia's and Michael's schedules well. She had asked her mother if Ophelia ever went by to see her and was surprised to hear that Ophelia stopped by on a regular basis—once or twice a week. She probably wanted to be closer to her mother now that she was pregnant. She was expecting the baby around the middle of July and was becoming nervous since she had only a month to go.

"Mama," Katerina said. "What does she do all day? I might want to see her sometime and want to know what her schedule is like. I don't know that I could really stand to be near her yet, but just in case."

Kyria Maria was glad to think that Katerina might be able to forgive Ophelia at some point. She had only two daughters in her life and hoped that someday they would be able to reconcile their differences.

"On Sundays she and Michael go to church and then she usually goes home to prepare dinner. That is probably her lightest day when she rests quite a bit. On Mondays, she leaves the house around 9:00 AM to do whatever shopping she needs and to take care of any other tasks at the marketplace. She's usually home by noon to prepare lunch for Michael and then she stays home to clean or iron or do whatever needs to be done in the house. Sometimes she goes for a walk in the early evening or goes to visit a neighbor for a few hours. The rest of the week follows pretty much the same pattern except that she and Michael usually go into Kymi on Saturdays. They both love to look at the waters of the Aegean, and it's so convenient that Kymi is such a short distance from our village. There they have coffee, walk around, take care of any official business they may have, and shop for the week in larger quantities."

"I see. She has stepped into the role of wife very well."

"Yes, she has. I'm not really astounded or anything like that since she loves Michael so much. For once in her life, she truly seems happy. I know how she hurt you, but I can't help feeling glad that she's no longer brooding aimlessly."

"That's all right Mama," Katerina replied evenly. "She is also your daughter and I'm sure you love her. How can a mother not feel glad to see her child content? I don't blame you for caring for Ophelia. I just don't think I will ever be able to do so again."

"I understand how you feel. This past year has been difficult for all of us, but it has been especially horrendous for you."

"Mama, how do you think Michael feels? Does he seem happy to you? Do you think he now loves Ophelia?"

"I think he went through a rough period in the beginning of their marriage, but I think he has adjusted. He treats Ophelia well and I'm sure he's looking forward to the birth of their child. He is a good and kind man. I had mixed feelings after we went to his house last September and I must say that I lost a great deal of respect for him. The right thing would have been for him to marry you, and I think he acted cowardly to reject you.

"At the same time, I have seen him struggle to make his marriage with Ophelia a good one, and I think he is a good family man. You ask me if he's happy and I can't give you an answer. I think he is doing the best he can to be happy."

"Does he still have political ambitions? I wonder because I know that he wanted to become mayor of Ano Kourouni." Katerina asked.

"Deep down I think he still is ambitious and wants to have more say in governing the town. I'm sure he has put those goals aside for now since they're expecting the baby. He doesn't seem as energetic as before, so perhaps he is rethinking his purpose in life. Why do you ask?"

"Oh, it's just curiosity. I haven't seen either of them for a long time and I'm just wondering."

"Well, let's forget them for now and let's talk about you. How are Giorgo and his parents treating you? Have they followed through in their newfound love of Christ? I heard that they've helped some neighbors who had money problems and I was shocked. Perhaps they are sincere in wanting to transform themselves."

Katerina, looking bored with the topic, replied: "They stay away from me as much as possible. If they have to face me, they greet me politely and formally, but I rarely greet them in turn. I don't want to see their faces, but sometimes I'm stuck. They usually go quickly into the house if they know I'm about."

"Has Giorgo ever attempted to touch you again?"

"No. He is obviously afraid of me. He becomes a little shaky if I look him directly in the eyes. What an imbecile he is! It amazes me when I now remember the times I was terrified of him. I should have taught him a lesson much sooner, but we all develop from lessons we have learned in life."

Kyria Maria was a little disturbed to hear Katerina speak so casually and indifferently about her life. Katerina didn't seem to want to do much with her future other than to make Giorgo and his family uncomfortable. That was very reasonable considering what she had gone through, but Kyria Maria would have preferred a response showing that Katerina was engaged in some goal, any goal, as part of her life. She was so young and seemed so jaded. It didn't seem mentally healthy for her to be so physically close to Giorgo and his family.

"Have you thought of perhaps opening a little business from your home?" the mother asked. "You always had a special skill with crocheting and weaving, and I know that many women would buy products from you. You do such beautiful handiwork and you could do those things at home. There are a couple of little shops in Kymi that would love to showcase and sell your products."

"I'm not really interested in that right now. With what Giorgo gives me weekly, I have plenty to live on. But I'll think about your idea. I do get a little bored at times and staying by myself so much may not be the best. Mama, you know what you haven't done in a long time is to read my coffee cup. We both know it's only for fun. Look, I'll make the coffee if you look at my cup."

Kyria Maria didn't want to read the cup, but she wanted to keep Katerina around a little longer so she said she would.

Katerina made coffee for both of them in the briki, the small copper container that could hold enough liquid for two demitasse cups. She mixed two heaping teaspoons of finely ground coffee with two level teaspoons of sugar and water. She brought the liquid to a boil and poured some froth into each cup. She then brought the remaining liquid to a boil for the second time and filled the cups. Plenty of froth showed at the top, which was as it should, and Katerina was pleased she had done a good job with the coffee. As was customary, she filled two glasses with water and placed them on the table with the coffee.

They sat across from each restfully and sipped slowly from the cups so as not to burn their tongues. The coffee was delicious as usual and Katerina made quite a production out of swirling the dregs at the bottom of her cup and then quickly turning the cup over so that it would dry and develop a design. This design is what her mother would read for her.

The dregs dried within a couple of minutes and Katerina handed the cup to her mother. "Let's see Mama if you can tell me anything more creative than you usually do. You know, I've gotten tired of hearing the same fortune for the last eight years. Please don't tell me again that I will receive a letter, that I will get some extra money, that I will sit at a table with people, that someone is gossiping about me, that someone loves me, and that I will take a short trip somewhere."

Her mother laughed and said, "Oh, so you caught on to my little game. I'll give you a slightly enhanced version this time." She studied the cup deeply and kept moving it around as if she needed to look more carefully, as if she didn't trust what she saw.

"Come on Mama. I'm patient but I don't think you need to look all day at a silly cup. Just tell me what you see. Start off with the letter and extra money if you want."

"Unfortunately, although I'd like to start off with the customary letter and extra money, I'm concerned with what I see here. This cup has a bad aura to it. I see meanness and revenge and more suffering. Hasn't this family gone through enough? What I see happening in this cup should never occur. I see betrayal by a husband to his wife, and shame, guilt, and regret. Why in the world this is appearing in your cup, I don't know. Look here and see the forked journey available and the consequences to each choice. It appears that the darker lines will be the chosen path and this will lead to ruin. The person or persons who are making the choice are aware they have two options, and they are going with the darker alternative of the two. God help them and us all. Katerina, what does this have to do with you? Are you involved in something unorthodox?"

"I wish I hadn't asked you to read my cup. I've brought you anxiety without meaning to. I don't know how, or if, I'm involved in this prediction. If my husband is with one, or numerous, other women, I don't consider it a betrayal. He may be with as many women as he wants. I neither care nor want to know."

"If it's not about your husband, then it must be about Michael. I can't imagine that he would have an affair at a time like this. Ophelia is close to giving birth and it would destroy her if he is being unfaithful. You may not believe this, but there are many women in our parts who easily play on the side with men other than their husbands. I was appalled when I first became aware of this, but I now take it as a fact of life and don't pay much attention. Oh, let's forget this wretched cup and pretend there is nothing there. Better yet, let's sing a happy song together before you leave."

They sang a lively number about love lasting forever, lovers missing each other, pledging to always be together, the hurdles each of the two would be willing to overcome for each other's sake, and the union of their bodies and souls. The song was a bit overly dramatic, but most Greek songs were. What they as a people and culture rarely detected in daily life, they romanticized and put into song. After all, happiness had to be found somewhere and music was an aphrodisiac in its own right.

Walking home, Katerina pondered the words her mother had spoken upon reading the cup. She was in such deep thought that she barely noticed Michael walking toward her, and she was startled into the present by his greeting: "Good evening Katerina. You look lost in another world. Of course, you look beautiful as always, but you don't need me to tell you that."

"No Michael," she retorted, "I don't need you of all people to speak to me that way. You are a married man and should be careful how you address women. If I were your wife, which I'm not, I would be offended to hear you say such things to others."

"I know you're right and ask that you excuse my carelessness in speaking so boldly to you. You are not my wife although you should have been. I am married to your sister but still have feelings for you. I say this and am ashamed that I say such things with my wife about ready to have our child. I have things, however, that I must get out of my system. If I can get these things out of my system, I may be able to better steer my life and my future. Katerina, I need to talk to you. Please hear me out. Please come out to the north field tomorrow where I will be working so we can talk at length and privately. You know which field I'm talking about—the one by the stream with trees that provide shade. I will go home for lunch and will return there at 1:00 to finish cultivating."

Quite astounded by his declaration, she really didn't know how to respond other than to say, "I will have to think about this. If I decide to join you, I will be there by 2:00. I have to say that I'm confused by your sudden urgency to talk with me. But, I'm also curious to hear what you have to say, so I will probably be there."

"I have much to say to you and more to say to myself," he said wryly. "I'm not even sure what my words will be, but we both need to put an ending to what has happened between you and me, and between you, Ophelia, and myself. We will be crossing paths until we die and we can't postpone this conversation forever. This has been eating at me for almost a year now and I need some peace. I trust you need that peace also."

"Yes Michael, I need that conclusion also. I don't want to think of you any longer. I don't want to get images of you and Ophelia together. I want to erase you from my heart and thoughts and will do almost anything to accomplish that. God help me, I need peace also," and she smiled as if mocking herself.

"Then, it's decided. We will meet tomorrow in the north field around 2:00. You can stay in the shade by the river until I come to drink water. If anyone happens to come by, he won't be able to see you because of the thick foliage. We do, after all, have to be careful."

Chapter Thirteen

Katerina scoffed at herself the next morning as she was getting ready to meet Michael. She was taking so much care in her appearance to meet a married man. Why? He wasn't and couldn't be her lover. He was her sister's husband and about to become a father. Still, she twisted her hair carefully and made sure that her dress fit smoothly.

It took her about half an hour to reach the north field by the stream. It was a short distance out of the village and she walked leisurely thinking the whole time that she really shouldn't be doing this. "You are a fool," she muttered over and over to herself. "Do you really think this will accomplish something? Well, maybe it will. If this puts closure to our relationship, it is worth it. If nothing else, Michael needs to explain himself to me and I can listen. Maybe hearing what he has to say will help finish this infatuation for me too."

Although she had nothing to hide, she tried to not be seen as she walked through the village. She didn't need to be questioned or to have people talk about her. She didn't want to lie about where she was going and thought it best to hide whenever she saw anyone approaching. Out on the road she stayed to the side and was able to hide behind bushes whenever she heard human feet or animals close by. There were shepherds around here and you never knew when one might be taking a flock of sheep from one field to another.

She reached the north field and sat on a large rock by the stream. She was hidden from anyone's view and felt relief that the thick foliage hid her so well. She took off her shoes and dangled her feet in the cool water that swiftly ran from the rocks above to the community well a couple of kilometers below. She could vaguely discern shapes of women at the well as they came to fill their buckets with water to take home. She saw some taking longer than others and could imagine the conversations they were having about fellow neighbors, illness, childbirth, and related topics. She was glad she couldn't overhear what they were saying since her name was likely part of numerous conversations.

Ever since she had turned the tables on Giorgo and forced him out of the house, her name had been on many tongues and a lot of what was said was not favorable to her: "Can you believe that she actually made him turn over the house to her? What kind of behavior is that for a woman? She should be ashamed of herself! And to think, she refuses to have him in the house and be a wife to him. I don't know what the world is coming to."

Others, however, saw the justice in what had happened to Giorgo and defended her: "That poor girl. What the ruffian Giorgo did to her was abominable and he deserves every amount of bad luck that comes his way. We now know that he raped her brutally before marrying her and that he continued raping her after the marriage. How fierce and pitiless his assaults must have been. She lost the baby because of him, and, she, herself, almost died. If her mother and Yiayia hadn't taken care of her, she definitely would have died."

"Yes," someone added in her defense. "Not only did she almost die, but she will never be able to have children. How would any of us feel if we were in that situation? I, for one, feel great pity for Katerina and can't condemn her. I only wish that she had maintained her faith in the Church and God, but I'm not in her shoes and don't know how I would react."

Her critics felt on safe ground when the Church and God were mentioned. Firmly and officiously they said, "Whatever happened, she should not shun God. She should not be dealing with the devil and putting curses on people! What if she takes a dislike to any one of us? Will she place a curse?"

"Come now," reasonable voices would chide. "Father Kosta has cautioned all of us to be kind to her. She is no threat to any of us and is going through great mental agony. She will find her way and return to the Church. We're talking about Katerina after all, a girl we've known all her life. A girl who has changed because of circumstances beyond her control. Let's not be so judgmental that we turn away from her. May God help her, protect, and guide her!"

Katerina knew of the conversations. Often, people would lower their voices if they saw her approaching or they would simply stop talking. She had made up her mind to not pay any attention to them, but somewhere deep inside she felt a sting every time this happened. Now, seeing the women by the well and knowing she was being discussed, she felt glad to be in the safe cocoon of the foliage. She could block them out from this space and distance.

She was in deep contemplation when Michael detected her through the leaves. He was thirsty but lost all thoughts of water when he beheld her. She was sitting so restfully with her feet in the water and her eyes dreamily looking up at the clear sky. She looked like an angel to him with her lovely and tempting body that was made to be caressed, with smooth clear skin that was meant be touched, with lips intended to be kissed.

Catching his breath, he whispered, "Katerina, I'm here and I'm already wondering if this is a mistake. I desire you too much to keep a clear head."

"Hello Michael," she responded. "That's not what I expected you to say. The more I thought of this, the more I realized we need to talk and resolve what has happened between us. I, for one, am glad to have this encounter. I'd like to move on with my life, however pitiful it may be. Come, drink some water, and sit down so we can talk."

He did as she instructed, slowly sipping his water so as to delay being too near to her. She became a little impatient at his dawdling and sharply commented that she would leave if he didn't want to talk to her.

He immediately sat and said, "Katerina, I've made so many mistakes and I can't undo them now. I don't know how I turned you away when you came to me. What a fool I was and how miserable I've made myself! You were the love of my life and I turned you away for my paltry ambition. I find nothing significant in my previous ambitions. I may still become involved in politics because I have to do something with my life, but the zest for such things is no longer there. I need you in my life."

"We decided to meet and talk to put things behind us," she countered. "What you're saying doesn't seem to lead to that. Are you trying to seduce me?"

"No, I was being truthful in suggesting this meeting. It's only that, now that you are here, I can't help but state what I feel. I can't deny my love for you and only you. I don't know what to do and how I will live the rest of my life without you. Am I trying to seduce you? Yes, I probably am. I need to touch you, to at least kiss you. Katerina, won't you allow me that small indulgence?"

"That indulgence is not small."

"No, it's not. In fact, it would be a great indulgence for me. Let me just touch your ivory cheeks and taste your lips. I have dreamt of this so many years and so many nights. I think of you throughout my days and dream of you in my sleep."

He leaned forward and placed one arm around her back. She held her breath when she felt his fingers caress her cheek and she moaned when his lips touched hers. His touch was gentle as their lips met, almost like a light breeze stroking her. She melted and wrapped her arms around his neck and drew him to her.

He unbound the hair she had carefully wrapped earlier and let it fall around her face. He ran his fingers through the loose, black strands and hoarsely murmured, "Even the full moon in all her beauty can't outshine you, my love."

Slowly, he unbuttoned her dress and kissed her shoulders and neck. He stroked her breasts smoothly and then more forcefully as she sighed with pleasure. Slowly, slowly he took the dress off her and she lay there in her underwear under his adoring eyes. His senses feasted on the sight of her, the smell of her, and the touch of her.

He massaged her breasts, held each one and sucked deliberately and fully. Oh, how she loved that. She told him and he promised there would be more. As he rolled her on top of him, she could feel how hard he had become and knew he would be inside her before they finished the afternoon. She wanted him inside her, but he told her to wait—that they needed to enjoy each other first. Michael stroked her thighs, took off her panties, and stroked her buttocks, alternately kneading gently. He stroked her inner thighs and felt her wetness. He had to taste her and placed his head between her thighs so that he could lick and taste and feel her tremble in desire. Knowing she was wet for him only made him want her more and he felt the passion building in himself.

She wasn't sure how much more she could take of the sweet torture he was putting her through. Katerina had not had this experience and was awed by the craving she felt. She tried to pull off his pants and shirt and heard a mild chuckle from him. "I can see you're not very experienced at undressing a man. Let me do that."

He stood and swiftly took off his shirt and then his pants and underwear. He was a sight any woman would have appreciated: tall with broad shoulders, flat belly and muscular legs. There wasn't an ounce of fat on the lean, athletic body. She had always thought of him as handsome but had not expected this sensual—no, straight out sexual— form of a man. She wanted him and knew she would have him fully.

"Let me love you," she beckoned with a smile. "Let's see if I can make you feel as good as you've made me."

Katerina started with his lips and worked her way to his penis. She kissed and licked and massaged him as he had done to her. She bit his nipples lightly as she took his penis in her fingers and stroked. It almost undid him but he only groaned and held on. He didn't want it over yet. She took him in her mouth and felt him shudder. When he could take it no longer, he pushed her away and lowered her to her back.

Michael looked at her with a glazed look full of desire and entered her. He thrust and she responded, wanting to keep him inside her forever. Their bodies became one and she wrapped her legs around him holding on tightly and straining against him. He came first but managed to stay in her until he felt her orgasm envelope her entire body; shuddering and moaning, she bit her tongue and tasted blood. She didn't care and screamed with pleasure as her body released itself violently.

They were both spent and lay on their backs on the soft grass. Neither could believe the intensity of what had just happened.

Chapter Fourteen

Katerina and Michael met in the north field regularly. She was happy and had a glow about her that spoke of love fulfilled. Her mother wasn't blind and immediately recognized the spark that had suddenly appeared in Katerina eyes and movements.

"You seem different somehow," she said to Katerina just the day after the fortune-telling. "You appear excited as if you're anticipating something. Are you perhaps planning on starting the weaving and crocheting business we talked about? Or, is something happening in your personal life that you haven't told me about? I hope this is not about Giorgo! Don't let him fool you again! No matter how changed he may seem, I don't believe in him any longer. I don't buy into his new, religious front; he is evil to the core and will never change."

"No, Mama, don't worry about Giorgo. I will never trust him again and have no intention of letting him near me. I couldn't possibly bear to have him touch me again."

"Well, I'm glad to hear that, but I can tell that something is going on with you."

"Perhaps it is the thought of starting my own business that has me excited. The more I thought about your idea, the more it appealed to me. I plan to go into Kymi soon and talk to a couple of shopkeepers there. I'll take various pieces as samples of what I have crocheted or woven and see how they respond. Since you don't weave any longer, would you mind if I take the loom to my house? I am truly interested in continuing a tradition we've had from the beginning of our history as Greeks. I remember Homer's legend of the Odyssey and get chills when I think of the love Penelope had for Odysseus. She weaved a shroud by day to only unravel it every night so that she could fend off suitors while she waited for him. What love and fidelity she had to wait for Odysseus twenty years. I think I would do the same for a man I truly loved."

"That you are interested in the business pleases me greatly, but I'm wondering if you are getting too many romantic notions in your head. I'm sorry sweetheart, but as long as Giorgo is on this earth and you are married to him, you can't afford to think romantically of anyone—even mythical heroes. You haven't been lucky in love, and the sooner you accept that love is not part of your destiny, the better off you will be. I hate to say these harsh words to you, but I must protect you from yourself somehow!"

"Mama, I have accepted my fate and am living with it. Do not worry so. I know of few women or men who have been lucky in love. Really, I have to say that I know of none. I hope that you and my father were the exception, but I doubt it. What is it about us that makes us accept fate so easily? Is it truly fate when we don't fight for what we want? Maybe fate doesn't exist other than through our acceptance. What happened to the concept of free will?"

"You know from your religious teachings that the Church believes in free will in relation to a person accepting or rejecting God. Free will does not apply to minor things such as when and what you will eat. I'm not sure exactly what we're talking about here, but I need to say that free will does not apply to choosing which of God's commandments you can accept or reject. If you reject the grace of God, you know that you are committing blasphemy. My Katerina, you are not happy with the Church right now. I know that and will not try to sway you, but I am concerned about your eternal soul. I want you in heaven with your father and me when the time comes. Please be careful in whatever you do. I am your mother and will love you forever regardless of what you think or do. You know that," Kyria Maria spoke decisively as she wistfully allowed her mind to drift back to her marriage with Vasili, her dear husband who had died too young. How they had loved and cherished each other!

Vasili had seen her in Church one Sunday when they were both eighteen and was amazed that he hadn't really noticed her before. They had lived a few houses apart all their lives and he knew her well. They had played together as children and she had once punched him in the stomach—not that he thought he deserved it. They had chased each other and climbed trees together and had done a lot with all of the other neighborhood kids until they were around twelve. Then, suddenly, they had stopped playing together. He didn't know why that had happened but just accepted that something had changed. He realized that it probably had something to do with her being a girl and him being a boy.

But when he saw her in Church that Sunday morning, he couldn't believe she was the same young woman as the girl he had known so well. When had she become so beautiful he wondered. She was such a lovely creature with a lean, softly rounded body and a clear complexioned face. She had dark hair that set off the creamy pale skin and the large green eyes. His eyes stayed on her throughout the liturgy and he made sure to talk to her after the service.

"Maria, are you really the little girl I played with when we were children? The one who, by the way, punched me in the stomach for no reason."

"There was plenty of reason to punch you, you moron," she retorted huffily. "You ate most of the pears we stole from Kyriou Thanasis' field without giving me even one. I begged you for one stupid pear and you held the bag high so I couldn't reach it. And you also told me to jump. How insulting was that? I was supposed to jump when I had equal rights to those pears. And you laughed. I had no choice but to punch you, and I know I landed a great blow. I hope you got sick and had to throw up!"

"Hey, I was only teasing you. I would have eventually given you a pear. Okay, I'll apologize now for being impolite to you. I hope it's not too late for an apology."

"All right Vasili. I accept your apology. After all, we were only kids, but don't forget my ability to land a great punch!"

"I've been away the last few years and don't know what's been going on in the village. I've been in Thessaloniki studying leather and shoe-making under my uncle Maki. I returned only a few days ago and will be living in the village but working in Kymi at the leather processing factory there. Could I stop by your house to catch up on the local news?" he asked hopefully although he was well aware of the local news. He had written back and forth regularly with his parents and was thoroughly up-to-date, but he needed an excuse to see more of her.

She doubted what he said about not being up-to-date on the local news and gossip but was also glad for an excuse to see him. He had grown up from the gangly kid she remembered into a fine-looking man. He was no longer gangly, but he was slim and tall with a nice amount of muscle showing through his shirt. He had light, curly hair that was cut short around his ears, dark skin from being outdoors, and deep blue eyes that twinkled even when his face was serious. It was hard not to be drawn to that twinkle, and she fell under his charm instantly.

"Of course, you can stop by my house. We're not strangers after all, and I'd like to hear about your adventures in Thessaloniki. I've been to Athens a couple of times, but I haven't often gone far from our village. You know how difficult it is to travel far."

"I do know, and I'll enjoy describing Thessaloniki to you. Generally, I enjoyed it but I also missed my family and the village here. I'm glad to be back among people I've known all my life. I'll stop by tonight after dinner and we can visit."

Maria was delighted that she would see him so quickly and went home in light-hearted spirits, humming all the way. She told her parents about her conversation and that Vasili would be visiting them. Having known Vasili and his family for a long time, they were very pleased. They doubted that he was stopping by to casually visit, but they kept their thoughts to themselves. Of course, one or both of them would be home that evening since it would inappropriate to leave Maria alone with a young man.

Vasili came that night and every night that week and the following. Both of Maria's parents stayed home every night since it was obvious he was interested in more than conversation. Maria's mother would make coffee for them and they would sip it leisurely, sometimes turning the cups over so they could read their fortunes. How they laughed when Vasili offered to read their cups. They didn't really believe him when he said he had a special talent with the cups, but they went along out of curiosity and enjoyed all of the nonsense he made up—always with the twinkle in his eyes.

On the fourteenth consecutive visit, he read Maria's father's cup first and solemnly looked up after carefully studying the design that had dried in the demitasse. "Sir," he pronounced seriously, "There is something special here tonight that I see."

Not having seen him so somber before, they glanced at each other concerned that he was going to give them bad news. They didn't believe in the cups but, still, bad news coming from anywhere would be upsetting. "Please tell us what you see," they cried in unison.

"What I see is that there is a young man in your daughter's life who is in love with her and wants to marry her. That man is the one before you now and wants your permission to have Maria in marriage as soon as possible. Would you agree to that?"

The mother, father, and daughter let out a huge sigh of relief. Maria's father looked at her briefly and detected the look of happiness that had spread on her face. She flushed. Imperceptibly, she nodded her head at him to let him know how agreeable it would be to her to become Vasili's wife. Maria's mother's face showed her approval and the father had no problem saying yes to Vasili.

"We are happy that you are asking for Maria in marriage. We know that she will be content and joyful with you, and we welcome you to our family."

"I have spoken with my parents about this and they also approve," Vasili announced with his customary twinkle back in place. "They have known Maria all her life and will treat her like a daughter. My mother even joked that she predicted this marriage years ago when Maria punched me in the stomach. Maria said she has forgiven me for the pear incident, but deep down I don't think she has. To truly ensure her mercy and prevent another punch, I've brought you a bucket full of pears that I left in the yard downstairs."

Kyria Maria put her musings about her dead husband away to better concentrate on Katerina. She reiterated, "My love for you will always be with you. Be careful with your life for I want no more harm to come to you. If only your father were still alive, I'm sure he would say the same things."

After a while and more conversation, Katerina left and Kyria Maria drifted back into day dreams about her beloved Vasili.

He had been so loving and kind to her, their daughters and sons. He had cherished all of them and made them laugh so often. He regularly hugged them, picked them up and swung them around. He was such a romantic, arriving home with wild flowers that he had picked himself. When pears were in season, he would jokingly bring some home claiming that he had stolen them for Maria. Everyone in the village knew the story of the stolen pears and didn't begrudge him taking a few. As generous as he was with his neighbors and friends, no one could begrudge him anything. They all thought of him as a spontaneous and witty man with the twinkle which rarely left his eyes.

He had that twinkle until Sophia, their third daughter, was bitten by a rabid dog. She hadn't bother to mention it since it hadn't been a major bite, and they had no idea that something was wrong until several weeks later when she started showing strange flu-like symptoms. She complained of feeling warm and also sensing a prickle where the dog had gotten her. That's when she finally told them about the bite. She lost consciousness a couple of times over the following week and scared them out of their wits.

They bundled her on their donkey and walked alongside her to visit a doctor in Kymi, only about five miles away but that day it felt like forever. They had heard enough about cases of rabies to suspect that Sophia was infected, but they didn't dare breathe the word rabies out loud. They knew that rabies would be a sure and painful death, and they prayed for a miracle.

The doctor could do nothing for Sophia. He wasn't sure that she had rabies and hoped that she was experiencing a bad case of the flu. The doctor was aware of a vaccine that had been developed by Louis Pasteur and Emile Roux in the late 19th century, but it was not available in the mountain villages. He doubted that it was available even in Athens, and, if she had rabies, it was too late to administer any vaccine successfully.

His sorrow for them was immense, especially knowing that he wouldn't be able to comfort them. He didn't dare give them any hope and recommended that they talk with the village priest. They cried upon hearing this and his eyes watered in sympathy. To lose such a pretty young daughter was a shame! To lose anyone to rabies was a crime he thought, knowing fully well of the pain and misery that rabies brought with it.

Shortly after they returned home with Sophia, her symptoms worsened. She couldn't sleep, fidgeted and was restless. Sometimes she didn't know where she was. She looked at her family in distrust and sometimes hallucinated, screaming out at the demons that possessed her. During her final days she had hydrophobia and panicked whenever anyone mentioned water. She was so thirsty but couldn't bear the thought of water. They saw her producing more and more saliva and felt her pain when she had agonizing contractions in her throat. They would never be able to forget her tortured cries and her anguish, but they could do nothing for her other than wait for the blessed relief of death, which took place nine days after the first signs of rabies had shown up.

It was a dark day for the family when they saw that she had drawn her last breath, but they were gratified that she would finally have peace. If the Church had allowed, they would have killed her to shorten her pain, but they knew that wasn't an option. They had gone as far as to discuss shortening her life with the priest and he had warned against such action.

"You cannot do that," he had admonished. "Taking a life is strictly prohibited by the Sixth Commandment which states, 'You shall not kill' (Exodus 20:13). I sense and feel your suffering as well as your daughter's. God feels it too and has incredible compassion for you although you may find that hard to believe at this moment. Have faith in God and know that Sophia will be with Him in heaven shortly."

So, they buried her and cried, and the entire village cried with them.

Even after a year had passed, Vasili wasn't the same man he had been before Sophia's death. He tried to console his wife, the two remaining daughters, and his two sons, but couldn't console himself. Of course, he understood that a lot of time would need to pass before he would again find joy. That was true for all of them.

One early Saturday morning, he decided it was time to cultivate the little acre plot they had on the hill high above the Church. He had meant to work on this plot for some time and just never got around to it. It was such a steep climb that he rarely went up there and dreaded carrying heavy tools all that way on his back.

"Vasili," he said to himself. "We have this land and it's a shame you've been too lazy to do something with it. Others would be grateful to have this piece and you need to stop making excuses. Just think, you can clear the area today and plant something next week. Maybe some fruit trees would be good. If you put in different varieties, Maria could store the fruit in a cool spot and we would have it throughout the winter. Some pear trees would be excellent and bring a smile to Maria's lips."

He had talked himself into going through the undesirable task and prepared to leave the house. As usual, he embraced Maria and nuzzled her throat. Their lovemaking had been sparse ever since Sophia's death. They regularly cuddled during the night and hugged often during the day, but everything had changed in their lives and they weren't ready to get back to their steady sexual intercourse. They knew that they would find each other fully again and were willing to be patient. The love that had brought them together was perhaps stronger than ever. Spiritually, they were more bonded than they had ever been.

He also kissed his daughters and sons affectionately and told them to behave themselves and help their mother with the chores. They nodded in agreement as his words went in one ear and immediately passed through the other. In chorus, they all chanted, "Yes, Baba." He always said the same thing, so they patted him on the head tenderly. What a loving man he was they thought. They were so lucky to have him as a father!

He sweated as he climbed up the steep hill and, at the top, he sat down to drink some water. He cautiously went to the edge, saw the Church below, and made his cross. Vasili took a deep, determined breath to encourage himself into starting what had to be done and inexplicably found himself hurtling through the air. In the few seconds he had before crashing to the ground, he thought of his family and said, "I love you all with my entire heart and soul."

Chapter Fifteen

Katerina and Michael continued their affair throughout the summer. They couldn't get enough of each other. The day Ophelia gave birth to a big, healthy boy, Katerina and Michael were in their little leafy home in the north field. She had arrived early in the morning and had brought a basket with food for lunch. Michael rarely went home for lunch any longer.

He had gotten there at daybreak, had put in several hours of hard work, but knew instantly when she arrived. He felt her presence like a streak of lightning through his body. He looked up from the field and saw her ducking through the leafy exterior. He had only a half hour's more work to do to finish the little stretch he was working on and hurried as much as possible with the anticipation of making love to her.

She was waiting for him and got up to greet him, encircling his waist and raising her lips for the lingering kiss she knew he would give her. "Would you like to eat first," she asked, "or would you prefer to have more a taste of me?"

"My taste for you takes priority. You're what I want and need more than I'll ever need food. Let me kiss those lips and neck a little longer and then I'll do much, much more."

She felt faint as he continued his kisses down her body and pulled up her dress to take off her panties. She had left the panties off purposely and sensed his excitement when he realized there was nothing to take off. He instantly hardened against her.

"Ah, this is how I like it," he murmured and worked his finger into her, driving harder every time he re-entered until she trembled, groaned, screamed, and came with his name on her lips.

He quickly took off his own clothes and picked her up so that her legs encircled him. With her clothes still on, he thrust himself into her. She wrapped her arms tightly around his neck and held on as she felt him hard and big inside of her.

She cried his name out over and over and moaned with pleasure. "I love and need you Michael. We were meant to be together. We are bound together."

"I love you too Katerina. I've never wanted anyone else and I think I'll die if I can't have you. I must have you. I need you every day and every…"

Before he could finish his sentence, they suddenly heard a voice from a distance shouting Michael's name. One the neighbors was looking for Michael to tell him he needed to go home. Ophelia had just had the baby and everyone from the neighborhood was looking for him.

Michael hurriedly threw his clothes on and jumped out of the shelter. 'What is it Kyria Koula? Is there an emergency that has brought you here in this state? Your face is too rosy as if you've exerted yourself too much."

"Oh, Michael. Everyone is looking for you to tell you that you are now a father. Ophelia just had a boy and is asking for you. She had an easy delivery so there is nothing to be concerned about, and the baby is healthy and yelling like a heathen. He already resembles you and will make you proud."

"I will be right behind you," he told her. "There's something I need to get first, but I will hurry home immediately. Perhaps you should splash your face with water before you return. Here, I have this cup and I'll fill it so that you can also have a drink to refresh yourself. Thank you for coming Kyria Koula! I'm very excited at the news and can't wait to see my son!"

As soon as Kyria Koula turned and left he went back to where Katerina waited. She had overheard the conversation and felt a sudden emptiness. He wasn't really hers regardless of the love they had for each other. He had other obligations and would need to fulfill those commitments. After all, his wife was Ophelia.

She looked at him and stiffly said, "Yes, I know you have to go. Congratulations on your son. I hope he will bring you happiness."

She didn't see him for a week after that. She missed him terribly and felt wretched. She wanted to touch him so badly, to have him touch her. She wondered if he would put her aside now and concentrate on his life with Ophelia. No, how could he? How could he touch Ophelia after what they had experienced together? She cried out his name repeatedly and could have sworn that she heard her name in return.

"I must be losing my sanity. I must be having halluci-nations. I hear Michael as if he's standing next to me, but I don't think he'll be with me again. That was a close call we had with Kyria Koula and he might be scared that we'll be caught," she spoke out loud, and, realizing that she had spoken audibly, was sure that she had lost her stability.

During that week without contact from Michael, she went daily to visit her mother and hear about the baby. She knew that the right thing would be for her to visit Ophelia and the baby, but she couldn't bring herself to go to the house. She didn't want to see Ophelia in the bed she shared with Michael. Her mother told her that they were going to name the baby Alexander after Michael's father and that they would have the baptism in late September after Ophelia had received the forty-day birth-blessing from the priest.

Kyria Maria hinted that Ophelia was considering asking Katerina to be the baby's godmother. She had been surprised that Ophelia had voiced such a desire and had gently tried to dissuade her.

"Ophelia," she had said. "You might want to consider someone from Michael's side of the family. This has been a tough year for Katerina and she's struggling with her faith in God. She might not be the right person at this time, but, hopefully, she'll be in a position to baptize your next child."

Upon hearing that Ophelia was considering her as a godmother, Katerina backed away and clutched her hands. "No, I would never want to be the godmother. I know this is my nephew, but a godmother has special responsibilities that I don't see myself able to perform. I am definitely not interested in being responsible for the child's spiritual upbringing. Besides, after all that has happened between Ophelia and me, I don't understand how she would even consider this. I trust her so little that I can't help but think she has some evil intent."

"That's what I thought although I don't think there is any evil intent here. But, I understand that you don't want to go to their house and only hope you'll attend the baptism in September."

Katerina finished her visit and left somewhat muddled. She had a lot on her mind as she walked home. Her mind whirled like a hurricane in all directions as she thought of the baby and the baptism, of Ophelia, and especially of Michael. She was so busy thinking of him that she didn't realize who it was when he stopped her.

"It seems that you don't pay attention to your surroundings when you walk," he observed. "This is the second time I have met you walking in a trance. You should be careful not to stumble over a rock or step into a hole."

"Yes, yes," she nodded still not realizing it was Michael. "I just have too much on my mind and am acting rather foolishly."

"Katerina, look at me. I'm Michael. You're so oblivious that you don't even recognize me." He shook her lightly to get her attention. "I've had you on my mind all week and couldn't decide how to best get in touch with you. I can't just forget you Katerina. Please come to see me tomorrow. I can't live without you. Seeing you here makes me ache to touch you. You are my first love and my last. You are my heart, my eyes, and my soul! God help me but I can't do without you."

With those words, she knew she didn't stand a chance. The following day she went to the north field and continued going there through October until it became too cold and rainy and the foliage couldn't protect them from the elements any longer. But Michael had prepared for that eventuality and had worked on the little shepherd's hut in the west field that had been there for years. He reinforced the walls and roof and strung a rod from one wall to the other in the middle of the hut. On the rod, he placed a thick curtain which effectively cut the room in half. Furthermore, he dug a small basement large enough to hold a couple of bodies and covered the area with boards. He brought in a little bunk and mattress, some sheets and blankets, a little table and two chairs. He thoroughly cleaned the small shepherd's hut and placed a lock on the inside of the door. It was nothing fancy but it was fit for human habitation on at least a temporary basis.

One warm and clear day in October, he took Katerina there to show her what he had done. She was relieved that she could continue to see him but was curious about the curtain dividing the room in the middle. He explained that it was just in case they had another close call with someone stopping by to look for him. Of course, he would try to head off anyone before opening the door, but he wanted more of a guarantee that no one would see her there. The small basement could be used to hide her if necessary.

Chapter Sixteen

October was very drizzly and cloudy that year. Usually, October was a pleasant month with temperatures around seventy degrees Fahrenheit. The rainfall had started sooner than expected and there were only a few beautiful, clear days that month. The weather didn't bother Katerina or Michael. They lived in their own, insulated little world and had enough warmth between them to warm up the island. November was also wetter than usual and didn't have many days of sunshine.

Katerina had stopped paying more than cursory attention to Giorgo and his family. She barely noticed them when they were around and didn't think of them when they weren't. So, the afternoon she heard the church bells ringing, she knew that someone had died but had no idea who it might be. There were a lot of older people in the village, and, while she might feel sad that someone was taken away, she was also glad that that person, if sick and elderly, would no longer have to suffer.

She had been out picking greens, horta, to boil for dinner and heard the death knell of the bells from a distance. The bells rang slowly and somberly letting everyone know that a parishioner had passed away.

When she arrived at home, she saw that a large gathering of the villagers was outside her house. She quickly ran to Kyria Sotyria who lived nearby to ask what had happened.

Kyria Sotyria looked confrontationally at her and conveyed, "A great tragedy took place today. Giorgo and his parents went out to catch some fish this morning and they didn't come back alive. The rain came up fiercely for a short time and capsized the boat. They weren't very far out on the Aegean, but the storm was too strong for them to hold out against it. The saddest part of this is that they had become good Christians such a short time ago and would have provided much more to friends and fellow villagers if they had been allowed to live. But, God is great and knows what's best. Of course, the good thing is that they had made room for God in their hearts and lives and now will have the opportunity to be united with Him."

Katerina was stunned! She was even more astounded when she grasped what the date was. It was November 29, 1920, just a year and a day since she had placed a curse on Giorgo. The curse had been for only one year, and if Giorgo was to be affected by it, he would have had to die by yesterday at the latest. Although she wouldn't have felt unbearably guilty if Giorgo had died because of the curse, still, she did have a sense of relief that she had had nothing to do with his death.

She inquired, "Is Giorgo's family inside the house washing and clothing the bodies? I imagine they are and that Father Kosta is in there with them."

"Yes, that's exactly what's going on. They've been here for a few hours, so Father Kosta is probably at the point of sprinkling holy water on all four sides of the caskets so that the bodies may be placed inside. He'll soon begin the prayer service for the dead. They'll leave the bodies here until it's time for the funeral service at the Church. With three bodies, it's good that it is winter and they won't decay too much in the three days until the funeral."

Three days later, Katerina saw the bodies transported to the Church. Everyone came to the house and formed a procession line, led by a deacon holding the cross. Father Kosta, chanting the Trisagion hymn, walked in front of the coffin with his censer, which was filled with lit incense, lightly swinging. The incense permeated the dense November air and lent even more sobriety to the procession.

The coffins, taken into the Church feet first, were opened at the Church. A bowl of koliva—boiled wheat sweetened with sugar, honey, raisins or other dry fruit —was placed close to the head of each coffin and a lit candle was put on top of the bowls. This koliva is offered to all after the service in remembrance of the Lord's words: "Truly, truly, I say to you, unless a grain of wheat falls into the earth and dies, it remains alone; but if it dies, it bears much fruit." (John 12:24 RSV). The candle on the koliva dish symbolized the cyclical nature of life and the sweetness of Heaven. Lit candles which were distributed to everyone and remained lit throughout the funeral service.

Family and friends returned to the house after the bodies were buried. A "Meal of Mercy," also called a "Makaria" was served. Everyone chatted and ate and said good things about all three who had died. For the most part, everyone was happy that the father, mother, and son had changed their way of life and would now be with God. On everyone's lips was the customary "May their memory be eternal."

Since the first piece of the mourning period for Eastern Orthodox Christians lasts for forty days, Katerina knew that they would be going through this again in a little over one month. They might have another service again in six months, but would definitely have one in one year. The relatives might have another service in three years and could have a service annually if they chose to do so. After all, they honored the memory as eternal and listed names of long-dead ancestors for the priest to include in his prayers for mercy.

She hadn't enjoyed going to the funeral service, but then, who does? She suspected there might be a few who went to know what was going on or to get a nice meal, but, for the most part, everyone went out of obligation and to pay their last respects. She had seen the many sidelong glances people had focused on her and she didn't blame them. Everyone was fully aware of her history with Giorgo and probably wondered if she was thanking God for releasing her from any contact with him and his parents or was truly there to honor the family. She wasn't sure herself.

Actually, she had to admit that she was there to thank God for her freedom from Giorgo and his parents. She felt a distinct relief at the thought of not exiting her house and having to face any of the three. So many times, she had opened her door and seen one of them outside and immediately retreated back into her house. She had learned their schedules well and did her best to avoid them. After a while, she developed the habit of leaving the house before daybreak and sneaking in after dark.

Katerina also knew that the villagers wondered about the properties that had been in Giorgo's family. They really shouldn't have wondered about that since legally everything would belong to her. She and Giorgo had stayed married until the end and no one would be able to contest her claim to the houses or any land that belonged to Giorgo or his parents. He had been the only child, and she was now the only one who could collect what had been his.

"Well," she thought to herself. "Perhaps my mother's idea of developing a spinning and crocheting workshop is a very good idea after all. I could hire any number of women, install additional looms and make a thriving business. It would be good for me and for the families around here to gain additional income."

Chapter Seventeen

Katerina no longer bothered going to the little hut that Michael had reinforced in the field. There was really no need to go there since Michael could sneak in and out of her house during the night. Usually, he went to her house about an hour earlier than he needed to be in the fields, and, for the most part, stayed more than the hour he had granted himself. They had joy in their lovemaking and spontaneity and only wished that they could stay together in bed for a full day and night.

This continued until spring had warmed up the air and she wanted to be with him again in the shady little grove they had in the north field. This spring was beyond lush with sumptuous little flowers dotting the fields and mountain sides. She smelled the aroma of the flowers and knew she would always associate that smell with him. So, she wanted to be with him in their private hide-away where all of her senses could drink in nature and him at the same time. For her, the little grove was still the magical place where they had united both physically and with their hearts. This was the place where she could all but feel his soul go through her and surround her and become one with hers.

"Let me bring a little lunch for us today," she often cajoled him. "I know what. I'll fry some chicken and we'll have a salad and some bread. I'll bring just enough wine so that we'll each have a glass. We can then take a nap and I can rest my head on your shoulder. Of course, I think a little more than food and a nap would be even better. Let me give a sampler of what I can offer you and only to you." Typically, she would then stroke him or caress him or kiss him with both soft and hard grazes. He loved it and could never say no although he was beginning to wonder how this love affair with Katerina was going to end. Did it have to end? He prayed that they could be here on earth together until one of them died. He had no interest in anyone but her and she felt the same way toward him.

But he had to ask, "Katerina, now that you're free of Giorgo and can remarry if you choose to, will you do that?"

"How can you even think of such things," she exclaimed with a sense of panic attacking her stomach. "Do you think I could ever want anyone but you? I have waited for you for so long and now you think I might be interested in another man? I am secured to you beyond any moral matrimonial vows or legalistic nonsense. I am only yours and, until I see something other than this same attachment from you, I will always be by your side."

He felt relieved and cursed himself for even bringing up such a stupid topic. Where had that come from? Perhaps it came from the pressure he was feeling from Ophelia to have another child. She had often wondered about Ophelia and decided right then to ask him directly about their marital relationship. She had to know if they still had any sexual intercourse. She dreaded asking, felt stupid, but she had to know.

"I know that you and Ophelia still share the same bed. I know that you see her nude and that she probably sees you nude also. Do you ever have any desire for her? Do you ever have sex with her?"

She had caught him off guard. Never would he have expected those questions from her. She knew she had his heart, so why would she ask him anything so irrelevant and probing. There was something so different between men and women when it came to sexual intercourse. He could be with numerous women—not that he was—and they would mean nothing to him compared to her.

He felt a little on the defensive and carefully thought how to respond so as not to upset her. The fact was that he had been with Ophelia several times in the last few months. He hadn't wanted to, but she had lured him during the middle of the night with her big breasts rubbing against him and her hands stroking his penis. He had been mostly asleep and given in weakly. Damn that woman and damn him for being so weak!

"You know that I don't want to be with Ophelia anymore. I am stuck in the marriage and can't change that. She wants to have more children and regularly tries to seduce me, but I've resisted thus far. She is a good wife and a good mother, but I'm not the man for her. I know it makes her sad, but I can't do anything about that. Sometimes she cries and says that she doesn't understand what has happened to us. Ii don't know what to say to her."

"Does she ask you why you leave so early in the morning or why you don't go home for lunch as you used to? Does she ever mention me?"

"Yes, she does. My response to her is that I have many things on my mind. I doubt she believes me, but I don't care much anymore. She was the instigator in getting you together with Giorgo and getting me to marry her. Yea, she also mentions you but I tell her that I know nothing and to talk with your mother."

"All right Michael, I believe you. I only wanted to be clear where we stood. If you change your mind and want to be with her, I won't understand, I won't forgive, but I will accept it. I want to be clear with you. As long as we understand each other's terms, we'll be fine. The main thing is that you yourself tell me and that I don't hear rumors from other sources."

Throughout the summer, feeling very content, Katerina, with her mother's help designed the workshop for weaving and crocheting. She placed the equipment that she had found, and paid very little for, in Giorgo's parents' house. She had thought that she would have a hard time acquiring looms, but it turned out to be a relatively easy task. By the time she finished, the room was comfortably crowded with five looms. She hired five women and sailed into her first entrepreneurial venture.

She hadn't realized how much she liked to plan and design. She was good with numbers but had never had the chance to prove it; now that she had the opportunity, she made sure to keep track of everything related to money spent and money taken in. She was probably best with marketing and enjoyed visiting villages nearby to show off her samples. She dutifully wrote down what shopkeepers ordered and what they paid. She had even gone as far as Halkida, a good three hours away by donkey, and had been lucky enough to be invited overnight at a cousin's house.

Her Greek was not that of educated Greeks, but she could read and write and made up small fliers that she had checked for grammatical errors by the local schoolteacher before she actually distributed the fliers in shops. She added a few artistic touches to the fliers and thought how much better they looked. She hadn't realized that she had an artistic side to her but thought that the fliers looked so much nicer with dried flowers attached to the paper. How exciting it all was, and she felt quite young and more energized than she had been for some time.

Katerina felt at peace with life. Could she really be any luckier? All right, she knew she couldn't have Michael on a daily and permanent basis, but she had adjusted to that and made the best of what she had. She also could never have children. That disappointed her, but she rationalized that she wouldn't really want to have children if they weren't Michael's. She didn't like everything in her life but no one liked everything. When she looked at the positives and negatives, she thanked God for giving her fulfillment. If she could just keep everything stable, she would need nothing else. After the hell she had gone through the previous year because of Ophelia and Giorgo, she was ready to prostrate herself in front of God and thankfully let him know that she needed nothing else.

She had slowly rethought her relationship with God and had gone to Father Kosta to partake in confession the evening prior to the Sunday liturgy and planned on taking communion the following morning during the service. She had thoughtfully made a list of all her sins and gone before the priest with a contrite heart. She had been as specific as she could and made every effort not to blame anyone else for something that might have been her fault. She took as much responsibility as possible for everything she had done against God's commandments for she knew that if she denounced others that would be an additional sin. She went to confess with faith in Jesus Christ and hope in His mercy. She had great hope in His mercy because she couldn't bring herself to confess her relationship with Michael. She knew that her lack of total honesty was a great sin in itself but she couldn't talk about Michael.

She prepared herself carefully for communion by reading the Bible. She went to Church before the liturgy began with an empty stomach; she hadn't had anything to eat or drink since midnight, which was the proper thing to do according to the religious teachings. Her head was covered by a scarf and her face was free of any artifice. When the time came to partake in communion, she walked with crossed arms toward the Altar where Father Kosta stood with the chalice but suddenly, on second thought, turned swiftly around before she reached him. She knew that she hadn't been totally truthful and would be condemning herself. Better to not take communion, she thought, than to show contempt for a religious sacrament she had believed in all her life.

Father Kosta and others observed her reversal and couldn't help but wonder what that was all about. Father Kosta had a good idea but decided to let her come to him eventually whenever she was ready and search out answers.

He would be there to support and guide her, but he knew that he couldn't force her to say words she was not yet ready to admit to.

Chapter Eighteen

Katerina didn't go to confession again but attended Church regularly. The ever-present incense aroma of the Church put her into a serene trance; the icons of Jesus Christ, the Virgin Mary, and the Saints graciously welcoming her took her back to happy childhood religious holidays like Easter and Christmas when there would be a feast and celebration following the liturgical service. She enjoyed the few minutes reflecting and praying for loved ones before and after she lit her candle. During the service, she delighted in hearing the priest chant centuries-old hymns and hearing the cantor's responses. She felt so at peace in the little Church where she had been baptized and had gone to almost every Sunday of her life.

The summer had found its way toward the middle of August and it was Sunday, August 14, 1921. The previous year the August fifteenth holiday had fallen on a Sunday, and, remembering the rape, she hadn't been able to attend Church. This year, however, not only was she in Church but she had also planned a special celebration for her mother's name day on the fifteenth. Her mother, named Maria, celebrated her special day on the same day as the Virgin Mary. Typically, friends and neighbors stopped by the house to wish her mother "Happy Name Day," and "May you live to one hundred." Anyone who wanted to drop in was welcome. Since the Church was also putting on a small celebration and the village of Ano Kourouni was holding its annual festival to honor the Virgin Mary in the Feast of the Dormition, Katerina had invited friends and neighbors to stop by the house after 9:00 PM. The hour was still early by Greek standards, and she knew that they would have a house and yard full of well-wishers well into the night.

She had checked with her mother about the invitation list. She hadn't included Ophelia and Michael on the list and wasn't sure how her mother would react. She hoped that her mother would not notice the omission. Ah, but her mother took note of the omission immediately and cried out, "No, this is wrong. We cannot exclude my other child from my celebration. You know better than that Katerina. I started with three daughters and have only two now. I can't stand to lose another! Please don't do this, because, if this is how it must be, I would rather have no celebration at all. I am a mother first, and must always welcome my children into my home."

"I know Mama," Katerina replied slowly. "I should have known better. I didn't mean to make you sad or bring you bitter memories. You have always been a good mother and deserve proper treatment from all of us. I was disrespectful and am very sorry. I will send a little note of invitation to Ophelia and Michael as I will to the others. Please forgive me."

Kyria Maria had always been a soft touch and, hearing the regret in Katerina's voice, immediately hugged her daughter. "I know you're not a mean or vengeful person. You have a good heart and will be blessed by God for your kindness. I love you Katerina."

Kyria Maria, Katerina, and the neighborhood women had prepared food and sweets for several days and were ready for the guests when Monday came around. They had made dolmades, spanakopita, pastitsio, stuffed peppers and tomatoes, salads, bread, and prepared souvlakia for the open flame. They also had plenty of appetizers including tiropitakia, olives, feta and kefalotiri cheese. For dessert, they had platters of freshly cut melons and watermelons. They knew that no matter how much their fellow Greeks had eaten, those Greeks needed the fresh fruit to settle a heavy dinner. They hadn't bothered making sweets because it was expected that everyone would bring something to the house. No one went to visit with empty hands, and, as expected, everyone brought something whether it was sweets, flowers, or a small gift for Kyria Maria.

Kyria Maria had taken extra care with her grooming. She wasn't interested in a new husband, but she was a woman after all and appreciated a compliment whether it came from a man or another woman. She was still young and good-looking enough to attract a man's attention and some had tried since her husband had passed away.

She dressed in a soft rose-colored dress that was modestly cut but showed that she still had a fine figure. It was open at the neck and covered her arms a little over the shoulders. She wore the only set of pearl earrings and matching necklace that she had. So, who cared that they were fake? Her radiant face made them look as real as she was.

She welcomed each and every person at the entrance in the little yard downstairs, bestowing kisses on each cheek and accepting their good wishes. Katerina could hear her saying, "Welcome to our house. Thank you so much for honoring me by coming. Thanks to all the kind neighbors, we have food and refreshment for you, so please help yourselves. This is an evening to celebrate and maybe we can get some of our local musicians to play some music for us. I know that several have brought their instruments and that Dimitri is ready to sing. When they begin, I'll be the first one out there and I expect all of you to join in. Ha, what am I saying? I must be crazy to think I can hold any of you back."

Sure enough, they ate plenty, drank retsina wine or ouzo, and danced their hearts out. Kyria Maria was the first one on her feet when she heard the musicians begin. She took a handkerchief in her left hand for the next person to hold onto and struck her right arm straight out and high so that she could click her fingers to the beat. The first dance was the typical syrto—eight steps forward, one step back, rock on the right foot, and start again. She was good! She added her twirls, her little skip, and teased a little occasionally with some distantly related moves to the belly dance. It was her night and she was going to enjoy it!

Katerina watched her mother and felt tears overwhelming her. Her mother was still beautiful and ready to fight for her share of happiness. She was going to fiercely grab and hold on to every tiny bit of joy that life would permit. She would never be defeated enough to easily step aside without an outright fight. This is how I always want to picture her, Katerina thought to herself.

Being so similar to her mother, Katerina couldn't stay away from the dancing for long. She had also taken extra care with her grooming and had put on a red, cotton dress which was sleeveless, V-necked, tight at the waist, and loose enough in the skirt to allow for easy movement and dancing. She could twirl in it easily and felt like a butterfly when she did. She had splurged on the material after she'd received her first payment for goods from her workshop; she hadn't had any remorse for using her money so impulsively when she had bought the material and, knowing how good she looked, she had no remorse now.

She joined the dance line at the back since she was the last one to join and placed her hand—palm side out—against her lower back at the waist. Whenever anyone joined, that person did the same. It wasn't long before the leader beckoned to her to go to the front of the line. No one tried to hog the limelight for too long by being leader of the dance the entire duration of the song, and once she had circled the yard several times, she, in turn, would motion for someone new to go to the front.

But in the short period that she led, she was superb! She danced with her heart and with love for the movement. She swayed, felt the nuances of the movement and simply let the rhythm of the music soak through her. In those moments, she didn't care much if others were there or not. The music was for her.

Katerina motioned to another young woman to take her place and was just as happy being in the supportive role of second; without a good second, even the best leader would be brought down or wouldn't dare make any impressive moves. As she was switching positions and handing the scarf over to the young woman, Katerina saw Michael and Ophelia standing at the edge. She hadn't seen them come in but their absorption in the dancing told her that they had been there for some time and had watched her.

Bowing to proper etiquette and not wanting to upset her mother, Katerina left the dance and walked over to them. She greeted them very politely and asked if she could get them anything in particular.

Ophelia, with malice in her eyes and spite on her tongue declared, "You know that you need to get me nothing since this is my house as much as it's yours. You obviously put this together to look good in front of the neighbors but they know you. I don't know why you couldn't have told me earlier and we could have done this together. You just always want the credit."

"Please, Ophelia. This is not the time or place to show everyone how badly we get along. This is for Mama, and she is awfully happy tonight. Let's not spoil it for her. If you want to quarrel, we can meet another time and say all that we need to say to clear the air. You know where I live."

"All right Katerina. I have enough to say to you that I will stop by to see you in the next month. I'll pretend for tonight, but don't think you have me or anyone else fooled in any way."

Michael, feeling uncomfortable and helpless, simply looked at them. He shook his head and walked away while they both gazed at his back with love in their eyes. They then surreptitiously looked at each other to study how each other looked. Katerina, no longer feeling that she had to be caring toward Ophelia, looked and thought that her sister looked frumpier than ever; her skin was blotchy and she was shapeless as if she had put on extra pounds around the middle. Ophelia observed that Katerina had never looked better or healthier; her hair shone, her skin was clear, and her body was the same smooth, curvy-lined silhouette it had always been. Inwardly, she raged at God for his unfairness and managed to calm herself only by the thought that she, Ophelia, not Katerina, had Michael. They stood next to and measuring each other for several minutes, then turned their backs to go in opposite directions without a further word.

Katerina had wanted to throw thunderbolts into Ophelia's face and had almost shouted, "How dare you, bitch and sister-betrayer, have the nerve to even look at me, much less talk to me as if I owe you something. You think I don't understand what you consider and what you're capable of? I didn't until two years ago. I found out then that you're a warped, ugly, jealous, and malevolent person inside. You were never attractive, but now your exterior is resembling the rest of you more. Did Michael have to wear a sack over his head to have sex with you? No, he probably just closed his eyes tightly."

Chapter Nineteen

The next day, Katerina went out to the north field late with food for lunch. She was surprised to not see Michael out there working and figured that he must had had to return home for a tool or something that he had forgotten. Since she was hungry, she ate some of the food in the basket, soaked her feet in the water, and stretched out for a short nap. She hadn't expected to fall asleep and was startled awake by rustling movements she heard nearby outside. It was Michael coming through the branches and leaves and she sensed him settling next to her.

He kissed her so slowly, so painstakingly, that she felt herself floating through the clouds in the sky high above and floating over the deep blue Aegean like one of the seagulls she often saw at a distance.

"I'm so glad you came back," she murmured tenderly. "I knew that you must have forgotten something you needed, and I was just going to wait for you."

"I need nothing more than you. You are the most important thing in my life. I simply have to touch you, to feel you and I'm enchanted. You enchant me over and over again. You are my one and only, my heart and soul forever," he tenderly murmured.

He undressed her quickly for a change and she sensed a restiveness in him. She didn't mind. He was his own man with thoughts and feelings she might never fully comprehend, but she didn't necessarily want someone totally open. It was exciting to see this other forceful side to him. She had seen it before, but it was rare.

She responded with her own longing and clung to him fiercely, caressing his body with need and desire. Stroking each other's hair, they kissed everywhere they could touch and squeezed each other's buttocks. He sucked her breasts and held them in his mouth, indistinctly moaning her name every time he came up for air. He looked at her despairingly and cried out when he entered her. His eyes never left her as he drove into her repeatedly and when he exploded, a single tear dropped from each eye.

She kissed him gently and dressed to leave. She wanted to get back to her workshop and arrange the basket she was preparing to take into Kymi to show the shopkeepers some of her latest samples. She told him that she was planning to stay a couple of days in Kymi and would not see him again until later in the week. He merely nodded and lightly embraced her.

She entered the workshop quietly and was surprised to see that two of the village girls were still working. How dedicated and hard-working they were, she thought proudly. As she was about to shout "yiasas," hello, to them, she overheard them mention Michael's name and remained quiet. It was wrong to eavesdrop, but she was curious to know what was being talked about in the village.

She sat on the floor soundlessly and gave them her full

attention. Yes, they were talking about Michael, but they were also talking about Ophelia.

"Ophelia told my mother how excited she is to be carrying a second child. She's always wanted a large family and thought that Michael might have started to feel differently. She's so happy that Michael now seems to have changed. You know, the pregnancy and birthing were so easy for her that she doesn't mind that part at all. I hope it'll be as easy for me when my time comes."

"How far along is she, do you know?"

"She's about two and a half months. She's missed two periods and knows she's definitely pregnant, but she doesn't know exactly how far along she is."

Katerina heard the exchange between the two girls and shut down all feelings surging within her. Very quietly, she slid out the door without even standing up. She went upstairs to her own house and carefully made herself a cup of tea. Tea was good for all things she told herself, and mountain tea was the best. Her hands shook a bit, but she involuntarily giggled at the memory of an argument she had had with friends from the Peloponnese who had claimed that their tea was the best in Greece.

"Silly girls from the Peloponnese, don't you know that tea from Evia is the best?" she repeated the question that she had asked then and laughed uproariously at their inability to comprehend such a simple fact. "Never mind, we'll let that slide, my old friends from the Peloponnese." She smiled graciously and winked as if she could actually see them before her at the moment. "I'm sorry but I can't carry on this discussion right now. I have to take a nap and then get my samples together to go to Kymi tomorrow. I hope to see you soon," she finished and waved to them gaily as if they stood in front of her.

She took a deep two-hour nap and woke up amazingly refreshed and in her right mind. She gathered her samples efficiently and packed everything she would need for a two-day stay. She often stayed in Kymi with her elderly cousin Angeliki who could barely hear or see. Katerina appreciated this cousin dearly but was glad that Angeliki didn't engage in much conversation and went to bed, or to her room, right before dark.

The next morning, she loaded the donkey with her goods, said good-bye to the women in the workshop and set out for Kymi. She could have ridden on the donkey but purposely decided to walk in order to think more clearly and to formulate plans for her future. She decided that she would have the little boy who lived two houses over take a message to Michael in the north field. She would ask Michael to join her on Friday for lunch but to arrive at 11:00 AM so that they would have time to catch up on news. She would have another little boy who lived in the opposite direction take a note to Ophelia telling her that they really needed to have a one-on-one discussion and that the time to do so had arrived. They could talk over lunch at noon, but Ophelia should arrive no later than 11:45 AM.

Upon returning home on Thursday, Katerina did exactly as she had planned. She had already written the two notes. She had decided to have the boy deliver Ophelia's early the next morning in case Ophelia responded that she couldn't make it that day. Also, she didn't want Ophelia to purposely or unwittingly let on that she had been asked to meet with Katerina. She had asked for an immediate reply and the neighbor boy was supposed to come back with either an acceptance or a rejection.

If Ophelia agreed to meet with her, she would then have the other neighbor boy go to the north field and give Michael his note. She wasn't worried that Michael wouldn't come. She had been away from him for several days and he would be eager for a sexual encounter with her. She had carefully chosen the right words for him and the message was clear that she desperately needed to be with him.

Ophelia responded that she would gladly meet and would arrive punctually. Of course, Ophelia had always been the punctual one, Katerina thought wryly. Michael briefly wrote back that he was looking forward to seeing her.

Katerina didn't bother with any major lunch preparations. She had bread, tomatoes, cheese, and olives and arranged all of these on a platter before Michael arrived. She also had some wine for them to drink and celebrate the encouraging outcomes her trip to Kymi had produced.

Michael arrived at 11:00 AM. Katerina chuckled to herself thinking how Michael and Ophelia were so similar in that aspect. They must have more in common than she would ever have suspected.

She greeted him warmly when he entered but kept her eyes covertly on the clock. She kissed and stroked him as always but didn't let him go too far. At the moment, she didn't want passion to overtake him.

"Now, when we're together in that bed you know so well, I want you to have endurance to stay with me the whole afternoon. I want to make love with you more than once. I want you inside me, filling me over and over. I thought about you so much when I was in Kymi and I missed you so. I don't think you want to disappoint me, do you?"

She gave him an arch look and moved away from him. He tried to wrap his arms around her five minutes later but she again managed to teasingly push him away. By 11:30, he was so steamed and hungry for her that she thought the right time had come to give him something more substantial.

She rubbed against him and felt him harden. "Michael, my love" she moaned. "You are my eyes and my heart. I can't be without you. Talk to me and tell me how you feel. I need to know how you feel about me."

"Katerina, you know how I feel about you, but I'll tell you as many times as you want. You are the only woman for me. You fill my dreams when I sleep and I think of no one else when I'm awake. I love you and only you. I want no other woman. Please, my sweetheart, don't torture me any longer. Let me make love to you fully."

He carried her to the bed and undressed her. As usual, he also undressed himself too. He groaned in desperate pleasure as he looked at her and then he entered her while whispering endearments the whole time.

Katerina had left the door unlocked and heard it open. She paid no attention to the creaking sound the door always made and focused her gaze on Michael. "Yes, yes, my love. This is what I want," she shouted as if exploding in rapture. "If only we could do that again, but I'm afraid someone is here."

He looked up and saw Ophelia. He might as well have seen death. He then turned his gaze to Katerina and grasped the truth in her bottomless pupils. He knew it was too late.

Ophelia hurled the first object she could find at them and cursed her sister unsparingly, without pause invoking the wrath of heaven and hell on her.

Katerina beheld both of them quietly until Ophelia ran out of breath and slumped to the floor. "Yes, sister," she said evenly. "I am all of what you say. You taught me well and I have now grown up. I expect no forgiveness and plan to give none in return.

"As for you, Michael, I must leave you to the life you have made for yourself. All I ever wanted was for you to be honest with me. You should have understood that you couldn't have both my sister and me. Please leave and don't apologize for I have become so tired of being asked for forgiveness."

About the Author

Helen Nickolson was born in Kato Kourouni, a small village in Evia, Greece, which had neither water nor electricity at that time. Sponsored by her aunt and uncle to emigrate to the United States when she was five, she journeyed across the rough Atlantic Ocean in December on an Italian ship. From New York, she then travelled by bus to Lodi, California and arrived on Christmas Eve. Her name in Greek is Eleni Nikolaou and was changed by her uncle to "better assimilate" into American society. He meant well.

After high school, Helen attended the University of California at Davis where she majored in English. She went on to graduate school at California State University, Sacramento and received her MS in Counseling Psychology and MA in English. Helen worked as a counselor and also taught English and Psychology at Yuba Community College for 30 years before retiring. She has been married for 35 years to Larry Michel, and Katherine is their only child.